Hypostasis

To Ellie-May

wishing you all
good things.

Brendon

Hypostasis

Brendan McCarthy

The Book Guild Ltd

First published in Great Britain in 2021 by
The Book Guild Ltd
9 Priory Business Park
Wistow Road, Kibworth
Leicestershire, LE8 0RX
Freephone: 0800 999 2982
www.bookguild.co.uk
Email: info@bookguild.co.uk
Twitter: @bookguild

Typeset in 11pt Baskerville

Printed and bound in the UK by 4edge Limited

ISBN 978 1913913 496

British Library Cataloguing in Publication Data.
A catalogue record for this book is available from the British Library.

One

Longhorne, by anyone's standards, was an insular human being.

He dined alone, slept alone, lived alone and he understood that he would die alone. It was not that he had set out to live his life this way, yet at every level of his being, he knew that he did not want it to be otherwise. Only behind the walls of his isolation, he had discovered, could he find order, peace and calm, and finding these things was something that he was hard-wired to seek.

He was not, by any means, a bad person. He was not driven or self-seeking; he was not offensive or arrogant. He was neither cruel nor demanding. He was simply and completely alone; all the time, regardless of where he was and regardless of how many people were around him.

Had anyone taken the trouble to observe him (and he had no reason to believe that anyone would), his life would have seemed barren and featureless, devoid of shade, colour or relief. He lived a solitary life without friends or enemies, untrammelled by affection or animosity. He seldom spoke and when he did it was usually to ask or reply to direct questions. His answers were brief, factual, contained.

He had no religion, philosophy or politics to espouse; whatever beliefs and opinions he had he did not share with others. He nurtured no aspirations and he harboured no regrets. He experienced feelings, but they were mostly momentary, extrinsic, it seemed to him, to the business of living. They skimmed across the surface of his mind, leaving little circles of mild interest or disquiet that rippled briefly before dispersing. He had no appetite for exploring them or for allowing them to sink beyond the outer-most layers of his consciousness. To his mind, not only were they not worth pursuing, they were potentially dangerous intruders to be resisted and repelled as soon as they appeared.

His antipathy to all emotion was part of a deeply rooted self-defence system that he had constructed, protecting the fortress of his isolation. Feelings were alien, destructive, unmanageable. In spite of his rejection of them, however, he knew that there was one circumstance in which he could not avoid them entirely. When he perceived the studied equilibrium of his world to be under external threat, feelings would foment and then begin to drill down rapidly and uncontrollably to compulsion, crying out for order to be restored. They would growl and snarl, spreading panic; inexorably and relentlessly demanding attention until they were dissipated by the threat being neutralised. Longhorne found this so exhausting, so intrusive that he would not entertain the possibility of experiencing any feelings at all other than in extremis.

If it could be said that he enjoyed anything, he enjoyed order and calm and those things that aided him in achieving these goals. And yet, it would be wrong to use words like *enjoyment* or *goals* when speaking of him; these might suggest a degree of choice or desire. Longhorne did not view himself as having either. He felt directed, though he did not know by what, to achieve order and calm in every aspect of his life. It was a necessity, a drug to which he was totally and helplessly addicted.

His isolation from people was fundamental to him, not borne simply from shyness or insecurity. For him, the lives of others *could be* of no personal consequence. He didn't actively dislike people, but he was unable, utterly unable, to make any connection with them for good or ill. It was as if they belonged not only to a different species, but to a species so alien that all but formal communication between him and them was impossible. He couldn't love, hurt, control, please or relate and he had no desire to do so. The people he met held no personal interest for him and he had no interest in revealing himself to them. He could study and understand the ways of human society, appreciate human history, but none of it related personally to him. He was without malice towards others, but he was also without feeling of any kind whatsoever towards them.

He acted in what many might consider an ethical manner, but he acted mechanically as if he had been programmed not to act in any other way. He did not reflect on the values by which he lived his life; he just lived it, obeying the law, paying his taxes and not disturbing those around him. He didn't think of this as being moral or laudable; he didn't think of it at all. He was entirely amoral, unconcerned with whether or not his actions were right or wrong; he judged them solely on how they impinged upon the calm order of his life. The actions of others were similarly of no concern to him, save that they were less predictable than his own and hence had greater capacity to be troublesome.

He knew that he was different, but he accepted his life as a hand that had been dealt to him; without question or complaint, without reflection or ambition. He had set routines, rituals and absorptions, but, if asked, he would not have been able to say where or how these originated. He knew that they must have come from somewhere, perhaps from his past or from some deep underlying principle in the structure of his psyche, but he had no intention of finding out. As far as he was concerned, they simply were.

Longhorne was by no means unintelligent, nor was he self-deluded. He did not shirk from acknowledging to himself the strangeness of his personality. He understood that he had a fundamental disconnect than ran through every part and aspect of his life. He recognised that it was there, but it did not trouble him. He saw no need to remedy it, reflect on it or regret it. He was what he was. *Who* he was, was a closed book to him; one that he had no desire to open.

He was satisfied to fashion his life towards one goal: his peace of mind. To attain that, he understood that he had to fill his days with some sort of activity, so he went to work each day, maintaining his distance from his colleagues, but being careful not to arouse in them any ill-feeling that he would have to deal with. He knew also that he had to keep his mind and body active so he read every evening, walked on Sundays and ate well.

His purpose was not to gain enjoyment from any of these activities, but to weave them together into the fabric of his life so that they would combine to give him the one and only thing that he sought: a life that was as emotionally neutral as it could possibly be. Even his desire to attain this state was something that he tried to eschew. He knew it to be there, but as with an embarrassing relative, he chose to ignore it.

Two

Longhorne was not permitted, however, to end his days in such a state of self-directed ignorance.

His unsolicited awakening began abruptly and began with a seemingly insignificant event; not that Longhorne could conceive of any event that intruded into the order of his life as ever being insignificant.

On the evening before his thirty-first birthday, he had taken the bus home from work, as was his custom. It was a warm summer's day and he had removed his suit jacket, satisfied that his white shirt and plain navy-blue tie still complemented his navy trousers and black shoes in a manner he found acceptable. He kept his sleeves rolled down and his tie firmly knotted.

The walk from the bus stop to his apartment building was a short one, three hundred and eighty-one paces in all. He always walked briskly, regardless of the weather, never pausing in his pursuit of reaching the sanctuary of his apartment as quickly as possible. As the bus drew to a halt, he knew that it would take him precisely four minutes to complete the journey. Alighting from the vehicle, he noted that he was about to walk this route for the three thousand, six hundred and fortieth time: he calculated that when he had completed it he would have spent two hundred and forty-two hours and forty minutes of his life completing this daily task. During it, he passed eleven lamp posts, five on the left and six on the right. As always, he counted each street light, each pace and each second as he walked, effortlessly keeping a neat tally in separate columns in his mind. He did not take note of anything else.

Reaching the door to his apartment building he took the key from his pocket and tapped it three times on the back of his left hand. As he did so, a speck of dust or ash (annoyingly, he couldn't tell which) landed on his left sleeve, just above his wrist. It was a blot on his crisp cotton cuff; small, almost insignificant, but nonetheless evident to him: an immediate affront to his sense of decorum. Uncharacteristically, he paused in the process of opening the door and blew gently at his sleeve. Stubbornly, the speck remained in place, nestling further into the fibres of his shirt. He blew again, more vigorously; it continued its resistance. A third attempt succeeded in dislodging it. It landed on his hand and he felt an instant prickling, burning sensation, almost like a sting. He blew once more and the speck disappeared, leaving a barely perceptible mark on his skin. He stared at this for a moment, then rubbed it until the discomfort subsided. He recognised his own foolishness as he looked around to see if he could spot the offending particle. Sighing slightly, he turned and unlocked the door.

Longhorne's apartment was on the top floor of a three-storey building, set in a quiet and pleasant modern residential area. It was a two-bedroom affair with an open-plan kitchen and lounge. It was sparsely, though comfortably furnished, without television or any entertainment system, but with extensive bookshelves devoted exclusively to works of history, spanning everything from ancient Athens to modern Zimbabwe. A large armchair, placed with its back to the lounge window, occupied the centre of the room. The spare bedroom, Longhorne had turned into a small library with floor-to-ceiling bookshelves leaving barely enough room to pass between the rows of books. His own bedroom contained a single bed, a bedside table and lamp. A built-in wardrobe, in which hung several white shirts and navy suits, completed the furnishings. The apartment throughout retained the original 'turn-key' magnolia paintwork, as pristine as when Longhorne had moved in just under a decade earlier.

He did not know his neighbours, their names or their occupations. Occasionally, if he met one of them on the stairs (he always took the stairs; two flights, fourteen steps per flight) or in the corridor, he would respond to a greeting with a polite nod of his head, neither emitting sound nor emanating interest. His manner was not disrespectful or hostile; it was carefully neutral in every detail. His neighbours had changed a number of times through the years that he had lived in his apartment; this had escaped his notice entirely. He did not look out for them and they did not look out for him.

Once, he had received a written invitation to a party from a young couple who had moved into the apartment across the way. Pushed under his door, it was written on a card embossed with pink flowers of indeterminate species. He had not replied: it had not occurred to him that he ought to as it lacked specific instructions in that regard. He spent some hours, however, sitting at his kitchen table with his laptop, trying to identify the flowers. Apart from ordering books and groceries online, he used his laptop almost exclusively for such research, as and when the occasion demanded. In this instance, although he was not at all interested in flowers or horticulture, the invitation had intruded into his personal domain. Nothing in his apartment was unknown to him, nothing was unplanned, nothing was incidental. The flowers had to be identified. They turned out to be a rather poor representation of *dianthus armeria*. Satisfied, he binned the invitation and continued to nod at the couple when they greeted him until they were succeeded by an elderly gentleman who died shortly after moving in. His passing went un-noted by Longhorne, as did the presence and identity of his replacements.

On returning from work each evening, he observed the same established ritual, though he did not choose to think of it in those terms. He simply did what he knew he had to do: eat, wash up, prepare his laundry and take a brief shower. He then spent the rest of the evening reading from his library, ordering new books online or, occasionally, researching things that had managed to invade his territory so that they could be identified, understood and neutralised. Invariably, he went to bed at 10pm; he would fall asleep almost instantly and sleep dreamlessly until, without need of an alarm clock, he would waken at 6am. He would shower again, breakfast, dress and leave for work promptly at 7.15am. On the weekends, this routine did not alter with the exception that instead of leaving for work, he would go to the library on Saturdays and to the park on Sundays, returning at the usual time. At both the library and the park, he observed his work routine with set lunch and coffee breaks. His reading in the library was divided into four sessions of equal duration while, in the park, he would alternately walk, then sit in silence, looking across the lake that was its central feature. He visited the park, regardless of the weather; in addition to his suits, he possessed navy-blue overcoats, scarves, gloves and a collection of black umbrellas. He did not know why he followed this particular routine; he could have adopted a different one that produced the same results. He did not trouble himself trying to find an explanation; it formed the framework for his life and that was reason enough for him.

On the night before his birthday, Longhorne retrieved his shirt from the washing machine, inspected the left sleeve carefully and, satisfied that it bore no trace of the troublesome particle, hung it in the small airing cupboard to dry. He set out his clothes for the coming day and retired to bed. At precisely 10pm, lying on his back with his arms by his sides, he closed his eyes and within a minute he was asleep.

He had a dream.

For the first time for as long as he cared to remember he had a dream. It was a small dream, lasting no more than a few seconds, or so it later seemed to him. It was fleeting, bordering on the elusive, but it was a dream nonetheless and it woke him from his sleep. It kept him awake, staring at the ceiling, unwilling either to replay the dream in his mind or to go back to sleep, lest it should return. He lay still, transfixed, until his inner clock alerted him that it was 6am and time to rise. He did so, hesitantly, going about his morning routine with a disquieting air of unease and distraction. His thoughts were not as ordered as usual; as ordered as they *should* be. In truth, they were not ordered at all; they tip-toed around his mind as if fearful of disturbing whatever it was that had caused him to dream. With the morning, he wanted to open his laptop, to research this intruder, but his clockwork schedule demanded that he leave his apartment at 7.15am. He glanced briefly, unnecessarily, at his watch as he walked to the bus stop and noted again the presence of the small mark on his hand still evident from the evening before; another intruder, another candidate for his laptop on his return to his apartment after work.

It was his birthday and in spite of the battle to keep his thoughts in check until he could begin to investigate the strange occurrence of his dream, he marked it in the same way that he had marked every birthday since moving to his apartment. During his lunch break, he went to a specialist stationery shop, the same one as always,

11

and bought a silver fountain pen and a dozen expensive correspondence cards with matching envelopes. He had the pen engraved with his surname and age and with it he wrote, addressed and posted the twelve cards. Each card, absent of greeting or signature, bore the same simple message: his age, spelt in capital letters. Having posted the cards, he wrapped the fountain pen in the front page of a newspaper with the date clearly displayed on the outside of the improvised package and dropped it and the remainder of the newspaper into a rubbish bin. Satisfied that he had fulfilled his duty, he ate his lunch and returned to work.

In the evening he forced himself to dine and shower as usual and then hastened to seat himself at his laptop, fingers poised to begin his research. He hesitated, not knowing where to begin or which of his intruders to address first. Research was something that he was used to, something he was good at; perhaps, if he had found a topic that genuinely interested him, even something that he might have come close to enjoying had he allowed himself that luxury. His research, however, never took him down that route. The task was always focused on something that threatened to disturb his equilibrium and the goal was always clear: identify, understand, neutralise.

The intrusion into his sleep, however, was an entity, *a thing*, that he had not encountered before. He wanted to close his mind to it, to research the possible cause of the irritation on his skin instead, but the thought of his dream would not let him settle. Where was he to begin in researching his dream, *his own dream*? He knew that he could find a copious supply of online articles on dreams, their causes, significance and interpretation; some scientific, some pseudo-scientific and some just crazy. Nowhere on the internet, he reflected, could he find anything that would address *his* dream.

Reluctantly, almost rebelliously, he accepted that his dream was unique. He blanched at the thought, but as he ruminated further, he had to accept that it was more than unique: it was *personal* to him. He chaffed at the idea that something that was uniquely his had intruded into his sleep and had disturbed him. How could the internet help him to address that?

As he struggled with his own thoughts, only one conclusion beckoned him: he was going to have to face this himself. The dream was his; it had invaded his mind and if he was going to be able to neutralise it he would have to track it down to its origins. That meant he had to go mind to mind, *his* mind to *his* mind, unknown to unknown. He could feel the compulsion begin to rise, the need that could not, would not, be denied or assuaged. He had to find the origin of this dream, nail it down and eliminate it before it intruded again. Once safely on file, it could be analysed, parsed and rendered harmless. First of all, though, he had to confront it head-on; there was no escape.

Having determined his course of action he was immediately assailed by doubt: how did he research himself when lack of self-reflection had been a cardinal, defining feature of his life?

Breaking from his normal custom when researching,

he rose from the kitchen table, sat in the armchair in the lounge, closed his eyes and thought. He was aware that he was sweating lightly, that his hands were beginning to tremble and that his heartbeat had increased. He breathed deeply, slowly then stood up abruptly, walked around the room clockwise then anti-clockwise and stood staring sightlessly out his window, suppressing a rising sense of panic. He returned to the kitchen, poured and gulped a glass of water, then another, forced himself to sit down again in the armchair, forced his eyes to close and his mind to focus, forced himself to remember the dream.

He invited the intruder into his conscious mind; it accepted the invitation willingly.

It was a simple dream, seemingly inconsequential and brief. Its beginning was vague; the images ill-formed. He felt that he was underwater, but he was not swimming. He realised that he was standing; he could feel sandy earth beneath his feet. He was crouched, almost in a foetal position, though his head was tilted upwards. The water must have been shallow; his eyes were open and as he looked up he could see the sunlight beyond the surface, just a few inches above his upturned face. He stood up, breaking through the water, and as the sunlight hit his face the vagueness of the dream disappeared suddenly and completely. He felt something bordering on ecstasy.

The feeling was unexpected, new, exhilarating, frightening. Above all, it was unwelcome, foreign and yet, it was alluring and somehow strangely familiar. He recoiled from it even as he felt an almost overwhelming urge to embrace it. Caught between fear and longing, his rational mind intervened to shut down the cascade of emotion. He opened his eyes, focused on his breathing until he had brought it under control. With an effort, he forced his mind to think, to reason, to question the experience. How? How could this feeling, this experience intrude into his mind? Even more troubling, how could this intrusion somehow seem familiar to him?

Longhorne's mind continued to wrestle with itself. He demanded that it stick to its task: to think, to analyse, to play the part of the researcher of itself. He scanned his memory obsessively. He could not remember ever being underwater; not even at a swimming pool, still less at a beach or lake, though he recognised that memories of his childhood and early adolescence were sparse to the point of non-existence. Nonetheless, he was as certain as he could be that this was not a personal memory surfacing as a dream; there was something 'external' in it that stopped it from being a true memory. Even in the unlikely event that it was a memory of some long-lost childhood experience, the question remained: why had it surfaced now?

Taking a deep breath, he closed his eyes again, summoned his courage and allowed the dream to break over him; not once, but again and again. Each time the force of it strengthened rather than diminished, the feeling of ecstasy threatening to swell to an uncontrollable surge of passion. He became soaked with sweat. He found himself wanting to stand and punch the air, to dance, to shout until hoarse, to ride the swell of this emotion until either he exhausted it or it exhausted him. He had never experienced anything like it before; exhilarating as it was he could not tell if he ever wanted to experience anything like it ever again. Eventually, just as it seemed to him that he was on the point of collapse, with a supreme effort, he opened his eyes and noted with sudden alarm that the sky outside his window had darkened with the night.

Instantly, he found himself empty, cold and disoriented.

A glance at the digital clock in the kitchen added to his discomfort. He felt that its red glowing light rebuked him: it was now after eleven o'clock. Confused, almost lost in the familiar, unchanging surroundings of his own apartment, he staggered to his bedroom, undressed hurriedly, untidily, and flung himself onto his bed. For an hour he lay there afraid to close his eyes again, afraid to sleep in case the dream returned. And yet, he felt its allure, calling him, inviting him, *daring* him to succumb to it once more. His mind engaged in a tug-of-war with itself until eventually, his body intervened, forcing his brain to shut down. He drifted into a dreamless sleep. As always, at 6am he opened his eyes on a new day.

It was gone.

He could remember clearly that he had had a dream and that during the previous evening he had allowed it to resurface and control his mind. He could remember its contents, but the dream and its power has disappeared.

He felt a strange sense of loss. He had not wanted the dream to happen, nor had he welcomed the experience of the previous evening, but neither did he want the issue to go unresolved. He was still no closer to understanding the origin of the dream or its meaning and significance. He could not allow that to continue.

Although time was not on his side, he decided that he would try to recreate the events of the evening before. He moved from his bedroom into the lounge, tentatively sat in his armchair, closed his eyes and opened his mind, but nothing emerged. He was relieved and annoyed in equal measure.

He was no further forward; in fact, he realised that he had taken a step in the wrong direction. Instead of finding any new insight into the nature of his intruder, he became aware of a new, unwelcome feeling. He felt the slightest of dull aches begin in his chest; not sufficiently well-defined to be termed a pain, but real enough to be *something*. It continued to reside there through his shower and breakfast. He stretched, performed breathing exercises, struck his chest with his fist, but there it lodged and there it stayed.

It was a Saturday and as he left his apartment for the library it accompanied him on his journey, continued throughout the day and was still there on his return; a further intruder, testament that the breach in the walls of his citadel was going to be harder to stop than he had first thought. He wanted nothing more than his day in the library to be over so that he could return to his investigation of the series of strange incidents that had imposed themselves on him, but he had to bide his time as patiently as possible, pushing away potential waves of panic as soon as they arose. It never crossed his mind to stay at home instead of going to the library; that was what he did on Saturdays: it was non-negotiable.

He began to feel that he was becoming lost in a labyrinth of dead ends. The dream was lost to him, reduced to a mere catalogue of incidents: the water, the surface, the sun, the feelings of elation. They were the constituent parts of the dream, but even as he recalled them he recognised that they were as far from the dream itself as were words in a dictionary from a poet's carefully fashioned sonnet. No amount of closing his eyes during his lunch break, visualising the scene or even trying to allow an emotion to arise (a hitherto unheard-of tactic for Longhorne to employ) made any difference. The dream was gone; the ache it seemed to have given birth to remained. He monitored the ache throughout the day, suspicious that it might increase in intensity, perhaps surge or migrate to other parts of his body. Meticulously, he noted its presence throughout the journeys to and from the library, during his reading hours and during his coffee and lunch breaks. It remained immovable, insistent, just strong enough to assert itself on the surface of his consciousness, its source just out of reach, rather like the distant chime of a grandfather clock echoing along a corridor and up the stairs to an attic room, he thought. Why he chose that illustration, he had no idea, but it seemed to fit the feeling precisely.

How then, he began to fret, after he had returned to his apartment in the evening, was he to remove the faint ache from his chest, to restore his equilibrium? He was not used to this inability to neutralise intruders, much less to having to admit that more than one intruder had slipped through his defences to lodge themselves *within* him. He could not pretend that the ache in his chest was something extrinsic; it was coming from his body. However he was to deal with it, he was going to have to address something that was *intrinsically* his.

He was assured that the dream was not his in quite the same way. He was as certain as he could be that it had not been based on a personal memory. Even though it was personally unique to him, its origin surely lay without, perhaps based on something that he had read. The dream was his, but the cause of the dream was not. The thought gave him comfort.

Now, as the ache in his chest persisted in making its presence felt, he was not so sure. Perhaps his predicament might be even worse than he had thought: what if the *source* of the dream and not just the dream itself had come somehow from within him? *He* might be the source; he could be the intruder into his own life, his own peace, his own security. The more he thought about it, the more it made sense to him even though he could not understand how such a thing could be. The familiarity he felt at the unfamiliar emotion, triggered and unveiled by his dream, could only mean that the intruder *was* himself.

As his mind raced, a further thought struck him: what if he was facing not only an intruder from within, but an *enemy* from within? What if the source of his dream was something buried deep within his mind that had lain hidden and had now emerged, not merely to surprise or discomfort him, but to attack him and his carefully constructed life? What if he was at war within himself and this was the opening salvo in a battle that he might lose and with it lose all that he had built over the years?

A wave of nausea broke over him. As thought tumbled after thought, the compulsion to retain equilibrium began to eat at his stomach, overpowering the ache in his chest, replacing the nausea with a deeper sickness. He knew that he was in danger of losing control. He scratched at the mark on his left hand that had now begun to itch, succeeding only in inflaming it further. In his turmoil, first at his dream and then at the ache in his chest, he had forgotten about it; now it, too, conspired to torment him.

He began to count, to count everything in his apartment even though he knew exactly how many of everything there was. Suits, socks, cutlery, angles, stains made by dried raindrops on his windows, everything and anything that would come to mind, he counted. Once completed, he began again and again and again until 10pm arrived and with it, as if by external fiat, came exhaustion and sleep.

The next morning, he woke, still with the ache in his chest, but with none of the signs of panic or distress of the night before. He had no idea why this was so and he was reluctant to explore the change in his mood further. Although wary of disturbing this state of relative equilibrium, he did, however, still want to explore the ache, its cause and its significance. He was assured, though he did not know why, that somehow it was significant and he had to resolve it if he were to avoid giving way to the appalling thought that there might be something even more significant hiding in the recesses of his soul.

He was grateful that he had a whole day to walk and sit in the park. The weather was fine and the forecast fair. He would have a chance to order his thoughts, to think about nothing other than how he could eject or at the very least suppress his invaders, one by one. Curiously, he felt something faintly approaching optimism as 7.15am approached and he prepared to close the door to his apartment. Tapping the lock twice with his left hand, he noticed that the unexplained mark from three evenings before had gone. A novel, unprovoked thought crossed his mind: perhaps, this would be a good day.

Three

His bus trip and walk to the park were uneventful: thirty-five minutes on the bus followed by four hundred and eighty paces to the park entrance, located at the edge of a prosperous suburb, just before the city gave way to farms and small areas of woodland. The park was the relic of a large estate, most of which had been sold to developers many decades before, but the owner had stipulated that one area, incorporating a generously sized trout lake, had to be left in perpetuity as parkland. It seemed that he had envisaged the city growing well beyond its current limits, but instead of progressing past the lake as he had thought it would, it had spread its tentacles in other directions. The well-heeled residents living near the park had ensured that planning permission close to their expensive homes was virtually impossible to obtain: their properties effectively marked the city limits. To reach the park, Longhorne had to take a bus bound for a neighbouring town. The route had a stop close to his apartment building; a pivotal factor in his choice of domestic location.

He caught the first bus of the day. As he knew would be the case, there were few passengers onboard and the driver had to make only a couple of halts along the way. Without having to look at his watch, he knew that it was a little after 8am when he arrived; he would have preferred a precise time of arrival each week, but the number of stops varied from journey to journey so he had to be content with a close approximation. As always at that hour on a Sunday morning, he had the park almost to himself.

He began his clockwise circumnavigation of the lake that occupied the centre of the park. The lake was still stocked with fish (whether or not they were trout he had no idea) and he could see one or two anglers fishing from the far side, under the shadow of some large leafy trees that cast their reflection on the water. The park resembled a small nature reserve more than a recreational area, with pathways snaking along designated walks between trees, shrubs and wildflowers. As the day progressed, occasional joggers would mix with couples ambling along the rough trails, but few children or adolescents came to the park; one of the reasons Longhorne was drawn to it. Park benches were interspersed along the lakeside at irregular intervals, but there were no picnic tables other than in a designated area close to the entrance; one part of the park that Longhorne was careful to avoid. Longhorne had never encountered any difficulty in finding a bench to sit on alone; even in the middle of a summer's day the park was sparsely populated by humans, though a plethora of small animals scurried in the undergrowth, intent on their own business. Birdsong was more prevalent than human chatter. There were reports that sometimes in the late evening or during the night youths would occasionally use the off-path areas for illicit purposes, but these were isolated events involving small numbers of adolescents who lived their lives on the margins of the mainstream; the popular choice was one of the parks nearer the city centre. This was of no concern to Longhorne, who habitually left the park in time to arrive back at his apartment as close to his weekday practice as possible.

Walking more slowly than he did during his working week, one circuit of the lake took him thirty-seven minutes to complete, followed by thirty minutes sitting observing the lake. He repeated the walk anti-clockwise, alternating this routine without recourse to his wristwatch until it was time to catch the bus back to his apartment, observing as he did on all other days, two coffee breaks and a lunch break.

As he walked, he was not oblivious to his surroundings; he knew the location and number of every park bench and every tree. He marked where various trails branched off from the one he paced that took him around the lake. The features of the park were unchanging and ordered and even the changes occasioned by the seasons held to their own regulated conformity. Here, he felt integrated with his surroundings and at peace within himself in a way that surpassed the serenity offered by his own apartment. There, he had to create order; here it had been given to him. His weekly sojourn in the park was his sabbath; no work, no reading, no countering irregularity or intrusion. The few people that he met, he easily overlooked; to him they were almost invisible. As he sat, if he half-closed his eyes, they disappeared completely. Why he went to the park only on Sundays rather than on Saturdays as well, he had never stopped to ask himself; his internal monitor dictated that one day was sufficient.

It would be misleading for an observer to suppose that Longhorne was in the habit of spending his days in the park deep in contemplation or lost in thought. Certainly, on occasion, he found it necessary to ponder an issue, invariably how best to dissipate the lingering effects of some intrusion into his life, but almost always he allowed his mind to go blank, his feet walking well-known paths while his mind rested. Looking over the lake, he did not muse on the disturbances to its surface caused by the wind or on the activities of the various birds that paddled near its edge. Rather, he absorbed it whole; the lake crossed over into his soul and somehow refreshed it as if he had submerged himself in it physically to refresh his body.

All the while, he was able to complete mundane tasks such as eating and drinking, putting on his coat or deploying his umbrella, depending on changes in the weather. He was aware of the taste of his sandwiches, the temperature of his coffee and the warmth or chill on his skin, but these were incidental features; the peace, the calm, the order were everything. Today, however, he had to sacrifice these most particular of attainments in order to address the ache in his chest and to reflect on the events of the past few days. Normally he would have resisted such intrusions into his mental oasis, but not on this occasion. The need was too pressing not to take full advantage of the day.

On his first circuit, he concentrated solely on the ache itself. He noted precisely how it felt: constant, unchanging, not quite painful or actively irritating, but present, pressing, as if a small weight had been attached to his heart. Had he been anyone else, it might well have gone unnoticed. He observed attentively that it did not shift or vary with his heartbeat or breathing or with any other movement of his body. It felt much as a slightly too tight bandage might feel on his skin or a very light blanket draped around his shoulders might weigh. Not, however, that the ache was in any sense superficial; it felt as if it was lodged within the deepest part of his chest, perhaps even within his heart, although he knew that he was insufficiently knowledgeable about human anatomy to know precisely where the boundaries of his heart lay. As he continued to monitor it, the effect, he realised, was not, as he had first thought, one of constriction. The ache was not tightening around his heart or gripping it; it was pushing gently, persistently outwards, trying to expand though it wasn't able to succeed. It was confined by some unknown constraint. Having analysed the feel and the effect of the ache, even though still no closer to understanding its origin, Longhorne mentally ticked off the first step in his process of exploration. The next step, he decided, would be to try to identify the nature of the barrier that was constraining it; that would be the focus of his first rest period.

Sitting quite still on the park bench, he closed his eyes and concentrated again on the feeling in his chest. He identified the ache afresh, noted once more its contours and edges. In so far as he could attribute size to it, he estimated it to be akin to that of a small child's fist. He could not penetrate the ache, but that was not his present intention. His focus was on the interface between the ache and his body. He turned his mind to the ache's borders, tracing where it was pushing outwards against his chest. Without difficulty, he could locate it deep within him, but he could not, with confidence, know which organs in his chest it was pushing against.

Having mapped its limits successfully, he tried to feel the nature of the barrier that kept the ache contained. Was there something surrounding it that was protecting him against it; a barrier that his body had constructed perhaps? Try as he might, he could identify nothing specific: the ache pushed against him, but he had no idea what created its limits; limits that seemed not to have changed since he first became aware of it the previous morning. Disappointed, he abandoned the quest and, as he began walking again, he turned his attention once more back to the ache itself. Perhaps, he reasoned, he had overlooked something during his first investigation of it.

As he continued his morning cycles of walking and sitting, he concentrated fully on the persistent ache. He walked, rested and drank his coffee automatically. He neither saw nor heard the few people that he encountered; they, in turn, paid no attention to him.

He began again from the beginning, examining and then ruling out, as he suspected he would, the most obvious potential causes of the intrusion. He recalled the evening just two days before, though, to him, it now seemed much longer ago, that he had allowed the contents of his dream to overwhelm his mind and commandeer his body. He recalled the physical as well as the mental and emotional reactions that he had experienced. Quite quickly, he became settled in his conviction that the ache was definitely not the result of any minor injury occasioned by his physical responses to the re-enactment of his dream. True, his heartrate had been raised and he had probably tensed his muscles, but not sufficiently to have caused this ache. In any event, the ache was too deep to have had a simple muscular cause. He was reasonably fit; a raised heartrate and a bit of unexpected exercise were not likely to have caused him injury anymore than an hour or two of brisk walking would.

If the source was not physical, then was it in his mind? Was this some sort of psychologically induced stress response, masquerading as a physical symptom?

The thought was unwelcome, but he had to explore it. He was well aware of the bouts of compulsion that would seize his mind when his ordered world was under threat. These, however, had always been relatively easy to dispel. His tried and tested formula of identifying, analysing and neutralising intruders had always worked before. Never, as far as he could recall, had they given rise to what he would term stress; their sojourn had always been too short-lived. The word *stress* suggested something more deep-seated, more long-term than the brief episodes of *dis*tress that he knew how to counter. Even on the few occasions that it had taken him a day or two to resolve an issue, he had never experienced stress. Once he had embarked on the process of neutralisation, he always knew that he would get to the bottom of the problem; he would always be successful. That was enough to close off any path that might lead to stress.

He recognised that so many of his routines and daily activities were designed precisely to avoid him encountering stress, even though, in truth, he did not consider himself to have deliberately designed them. They had built up over the years, organically, it seemed to him. His mind had responded and adapted to the external world to keep itself in a state of general equilibrium just as his body adapted to changes in the ambient temperature. In reliving his dream, he had faced his intruder, had laid it bare and even though he had not fathomed its source, that ought to have been enough to have assured him that he was on the right pathway. He acknowledged that this particular conundrum might be more difficult to solve than most, but having begun the journey, he should have felt the beginning of relief, not stress.

The more he thought about it, the more he came to believe that the ache in his chest was *not* a symptom of stress. The ache was certainly demanding his attention and he was absorbed in addressing it, but he could not say that he felt any mental tension as he did so. True, his thoughts were intense, but they were not disquieting. He recalled that as he had left his apartment that morning, he had felt vaguely optimistic about the day ahead. Walking around the lake now, that same, gently positive feeling persisted in spite of his concentrated efforts to illuminate the nature of his chest-ache. He felt none of the familiar precursors of compulsion rising within him again, none of the feelings that he had battled against the evening before; he felt no sense of threat. He could not say that he was at peace, but he had moved away from, rather than closer to, the torment and turmoil he had endured before. So, he concluded, whatever it was that was causing the ache, he did not believe that it was stress.

It was during his lunch break, taken on a bench in the shade of trees across the lake from where the anglers had stood earlier in the morning, that a realisation, a *revelation*, began to grow as he checked his thinking once more. The ache did not feel to him to have an external source because it hadn't got one. That much was right; self-evidently right, he felt. The cause was internal, as he had, indeed, thought the night before, but not, as he had then feared, because there was something wrong with him. He was not attacking himself, nor was something in his subconscious rising up to rebuke him or intrude into the peace and order of his life. Quite the opposite was the case: something inside him had risen up to *add* to his wellbeing, not to threaten or diminish it.

He could not identify why this thought had come to him; it simply had. Once it had lodged itself in his mind, however, it refused to budge. The ache was a harbinger of something good, something positive; not something to be feared or even neutralised. It was pressing outwards into his chest, not because it wanted to invade him as an intruder, but because it wanted to *complete* him. The cause of the ache *was* something intrinsic to him, but something that hitherto he had been unaware of. It wasn't a new thing, it was something that had lain dormant and had been awakened; something he had now become aware of it, something that he had discovered.

Perhaps it had discovered him. He assured himself that it was not that something inside him had changed, not even something that had changed for the better. That assurance was important, essential to his mental wellbeing; he could not countenance the idea of change at any level. That would be a negation of all that he had established in his life. He was still the same person, *the precise same person*, he was before the ache took up residence within. He began to realise that he had to be more accurate still, more precise: while it might be right to say that the ache had taken up residence, the *cause* of the ache had not: he was its natural home. Whatever the cause of the ache was, it was not merely something for him to acknowledge or even embrace as one might embrace a visitor or a friend; it was something for him to *own*. It was part of him; in some fundamental way, it *was* him. It had to be if he were to avoid the conclusion that something in him had changed.

He was aware that this was not something that he could demonstrate by force of logic, nor could he present a rational argument to himself that his insight must be correct. It was intuitive, almost visceral. This, however, did not surprise him. In spite of having excellent analytic powers, he had long recognised that very many aspects of his life were not conducive to investigation, still less control, by his rational mind. He accepted that his compulsive need for order and calm might have, *must have*, a rational explanation, but the nature and origins of the need went deeper than his rational mind could fathom. Similarly, he did not determine rationally which routines and rituals to adopt to bolster and protect his orderly world; they were more like complex psychological tics than carefully planned stratagems. His various appetites were not chosen or fashioned by him; they were just there. Even his fascination with history was not something that he had nurtured; it simply was.

He had no difficulty, therefore, in settling firmly on the conclusion his intuition was pushing him to embrace. In a moment of revelation and relief, he welcomed the presence of the ache, he absorbed it, internalised it. It was now an intrinsic part of who and what he was because it was evidence of a benign part of his mind that had been closed to him, but which now had begun to exert itself as a positive influence; it would add to, not detract from, the peace and order of his world.

This unconditional acceptance of something that had initially perturbed him, was not a course of action that he took lightly. He knew that he would never have embraced it if he had harboured any lingering suspicions that the ache in his chest and its underlying cause were indeed intruders from the outside world. Had that been the case, he would have pursued his normal methodology of identifying, understanding and neutralising them as he did all unwelcome external influences. He was, however, certain that he was right, even though he did not know *why* he knew he was right. Nonetheless, now that he had accepted that the ache was something intrinsic to him, his response was very much in keeping with his usual practice. His ultimate goal was always to restore his emotional and mental equilibrium. On rare occasions, once he became aware of the existence of new internal realities that he could not deny, he would accept and embrace them instantly and totally. To do otherwise would be to invite further internal conflict rather than to resolve it. Thankfully, he seldom had to undertake this task and once it was completed he erased it from his mind and memory. Whatever new thing he had absorbed became, in his mind, part of whom and what he had always been.

As he finished his lunch, he felt energised by his revelation. Already, he began to feel that the order of his life was being re-established. More than that, he felt that it was being re-established on firmer ground than before. It seemed to him that he was breathing a little easier, that already, his mind felt a little lighter. As yet, he still did not know the source of the ache and he knew that he would have to explore that issue further in order to complete his journey of the past few days, but the thought did not cloud his mind or darken his mood. Intuitively, he knew that it belonged within him. He did not have to fight it as an intruder into his world, because it was not, had never been, an intruder. His panic of the night before had been for nothing.

Soon, he took the next crucial step in naturalising rather than neutralising his experience. He allowed himself to feel the ache once more, this time, not as an intruder or a stranger, but as an integral part of himself. It felt natural, welcome, at home within him. As he embraced it, it began to fade. It no longer pressed against his chest, trying to expand beyond its narrow confines. The boundary that had kept it from merging with him, *into him*, had disappeared. The source of the ache, whatever it was, had been assimilated into his body, into his mind, into his soul. There could no longer be an ache because there no longer was any barrier between the source and himself. The source was not only part of him, it infused him, filling every part of his body and mind.

With a sigh of satisfaction, he hailed a further moment of revelation: the source infused him because it was none other than *himself*. He embraced this new truth as fully and as readily as he had embraced his initial breakthrough. He had been awakened to the reality that his own mind, his own heart had pushed through the barriers of his everyday existence to let him know that behind the mundane world of his ordered activity there lay something deep and rich and *peaceful*. His peace of mind and the order of his world did not depend solely on him satisfying his rituals and observations; it was undergirded by something strong within him: himself.

He need not trouble himself to think about it any further or to try to find out what it was about himself that now acted as a guarantor of his peace of mind. That would be to open up the possibility of disturbing his newly restored sense of balance. He would simply leave things as they were and return to his life as before.

He had a vague sense that he had been here before, that this was not the first time that he had undergone such an assimilation, such an integration of himself, but his mind had effectively covered over such incidents. In a remarkably short space of time, this new experience would, itself, be assimilated and he would go about his life as if it had never happened. Total order would be restored.

One final thing remained to be put in its place: the dream. As the afternoon wore on, he devoted the final circuit of the lake to thinking about it. Before he was three quarters of the way around, he had managed to come to a satisfactory conclusion; one that now seemed to him to be self-evident, if a little convoluted.

The dream, he reasoned with himself, had been his *brain's* way of telling him that he had to become aware of the source of the ache that later arose in his chest. The source of the dream and the source of the ache were one and the same: a subconscious level of his mind, one that wanted to be recognised because of the added peace and stability that recognition would bring. The dream had not caused the ache, as he had first suspected. Rather his brain and body were working in tandem; the former conjuring the dream and the latter the ache. Both had the same purpose: to alert him to their common source.

The dream was not a symptom of an unease that had to be addressed as he had first feared; it was an effect, not a cause. Who knew how long the source had been trying to get his attention? How long had it been trying to get him to realise that his deeper self was there, undergirding and guaranteeing a peace that he had assumed had to be manufactured? No wonder that the dream had been imposed upon him by his brain; weary, no doubt, at trying to get him to wake up to the reality within. It was natural, inevitable that at some point it would grow impatient at his conscious mind's inattention. The remarkable thing, if any, was that it had taken so long for this to happen. Perhaps other strategies had been attempted previously and the dream was a recourse of last resort.

As he continued to think about it, recounting the elements of the dream, it made perfect sense that this realisation would feel like emerging into the sunlight after being underwater; no wonder that he had been flooded by feelings of elation. It was simply his brain's way of prompting him to pay attention; how could he have been so blind to what was blindingly obvious?

Having established the nature of the ache, the dream and their common source, Longhorne gave them no further thought as he walked towards the park entrance to begin his journey back to his apartment. They were now accepted and trusted parts of his world and he need not consider them any more than he need consider his compulsion for counting. He could discard them from his thoughts; he had laid bare their genesis and its purpose. At last, it all made sense and as he made his way back to the city on the bus, he did so with his order and calm not merely restored, but positively enhanced. Already he began to feel all the turmoil of the previous days recede into the distance; soon it would be gone entirely: he had solved the conundrum.

He was totally unaware how tortured his thinking had been and how unconvincing it would have seemed to anyone other than himself.

Four

It happened again just six days later; not once, but repeatedly. This time it was not a dream but something even more intrusive that shattered his concentration as he sat reading in the library. He had just begun an enforced week-long vacation. The company he worked for had a policy of allocating its employees their statutory holidays randomly if they had not booked specific days off work. Longhorne did not take vacations and had no interest in applying for leave, so it was a matter of no import to him when his allocation fell. This year it had fallen during the summer, but he would have shown the same indifference had it been any other time of the year. Consequently, he had left the building the evening before at his regular time to begin his period of absence. As usual, he had not said anything to anyone as he departed and, as usual, no one had spoken to him. It was unlikely that his absence would be noted.

He was not to know then that he was never to set foot in the building again.

Regardless of being on leave, Longhorne had no intention of making any changes to his weekend routine. He followed his usual Saturday morning practice, rising as always at 6am, leaving his apartment at 7.15am and making his way by bus to the city centre and the library. As always, he was among the first to arrive and was able to occupy his usual seat before other readers began to filter into his designated reading room.

The book he was reading was a densely written tome, detailing the life of Andreas Palaiologos, the last claimant to the throne of the Byzantine Empire. Andreas had led a colourful life, but no one would have guessed this from the dry prose of the account through which Longhorne was labouring. Not surprisingly, he was the first person to have lifted the book from its place in the library's late-medieval history section for many years. He had just concluded the third stifling chapter, barely resisting the temptation to yawn, when instead of seeing the pages of the book in front of him, he saw his hands holding what appeared to be a different document. The event was so brief that he blinked, thinking that his eyes had momentarily gone out of focus. Shaking his head briskly and taking a few deep breaths, he continued with his reading. A few pages later the same image was before him again; this time it lasted a few seconds. He screwed up his eyes, opened and shut them a few times, and looked around to see if anyone had observed this uncharacteristic behaviour. He was sitting in a single cubicle, one of a series in a row squeezed between the bookshelves and the left wall of the room; only someone walking past could have noted his actions. This particular Saturday morning the library was far from busy; fortunately, there was no one around to observe him.

He cleared his throat as if to dislodge an obstruction, aware that his saliva had thickened. In a moment, his mouth had gone dry. A quick stab of panic ran through his body and shot into his brain. He took a few slow, deep breaths and he felt the panic slowly subside. Perhaps his mind had drifted or he had nodded off for a moment; after all, the book was hard going even for him. That, he thought, must be it. He glanced at his watch, an action that he only performed when he felt under pressure, and saw that he had an hour to go before his scheduled coffee break. For the briefest of moments, he considered abandoning the inflexibility of his pre-ordained schedule, but dismissed the thought instantly: it was too much a part of his ordered world to be toyed with. Instead, he removed his jacket, although the library was not warm, its temperature being kept just a little on the cool side of standard room temperature as an aid to readers who required to stay alert as they read or researched. Immediately he felt a little better and he settled back uneasily to his book, slowly composing himself. Nothing further unusual happened before his coffee break or between coffee and lunch. He determined to push the unusual incidents from his mind until he was able to research them later that evening in his apartment.

He was half an hour into his second afternoon session when it returned. This time it lasted for more than a minute, disturbing much more than his vision. He had time to notice in greater detail, both the document and the hands holding it. The document appeared to be superimposed on the pages of his book, yellowed with age and semi-translucent, enabling him to see the outline of the text of his book underneath. Nonetheless, he could clearly see the lettering on the document though this was, at first, indecipherable. The words did not appear to be English; in fact they did not appear to be written in Latin script. He thought that he recognised some of the symbols, but they were hand-written and ran into one another in unbroken lines. His examination of them was cut short as his gaze fell on the hands that framed the book. They *were* his hands, he could feel them as part of his body, but they were not pale and lightly freckled, they were dark, much darker than his hands could ever be. There were no signs of freckles and they seemed stronger, thicker than the hands that a few moments before had held only the book on Byzantium's last Pretender.

Even as he took in these features, he heard himself reading aloud in a clear voice; again, the voice *was* his, but it did not have his tone or timbre. It was deeper, fuller than his normal speaking voice, with a rougher edge. He understood what he was saying and he recognised that the words that were coming out of his mouth were words from the yellowed document. He was, however, neither reading nor thinking in English. He was not mentally translating the document, however quickly, from some foreign language into English; he understood it instinctively as if this unknown script and the language it was written in were his own, had always been his own. As he read, clearly and confidently, he had an overwhelming sense of peace, calm and order. He was completely in control of himself and his environment: everything was as it was meant to be.

As abruptly as it had begun, it ended: he was sitting at his desk as he had been a few moments earlier, the tedious chronicle of Andreas Palaiologos open before him. No one in the library had shifted their gaze to him; no inquisitive eyes stared above the cubicle partitions in his direction. No one shushed him. Whatever had happened, had happened in his own consciousness alone. His voice had not been raised in proclamation; no words had passed his lips.

Longhorne dropped his book on the desk in front of him as if it had burst into flames. Aghast, he stared at it, stared at his hands and then examined the book again. The book was just a book; his hands were just his hands. In a reflex movement, he raised a hand to his throat, the throat that had emitted the strange sounds; with his index finger he touched his lips, the lips that had formed this unknown, yet puzzlingly familiar, tongue. The room began to swirl around him, a persistent buzzing rose and then gave way to an insistent ringing in his ears, his vision narrowed to a tunnel that grew darker by the second. He felt consciousness draining from him. With a supreme effort, he barked a command to himself, forced the tunnel to widen, the darkness to disperse and the ringing to cease. He shook his head vigorously, gasped his lungs full of air and willed his eyes to focus on the discarded book. It lay there innocuously, holding no secrets or surprises save the catalogue of Andreas's closing years. Tentatively, his heart still pounding, he stretched out his hand to touch it. It remained unaltered. He grasped it boldly with both hands, opened its pages, made himself find the page he had been reading and commanded himself to look at the passage. He winced, expecting and fearing that he might be hurled back into the other world of the aged document. Andreas, it seemed, was contemplating selling his imperial title and rights to Charles VII of France. Longhorne felt like crying with relief as he scanned the pages, any interest in its subject gone forever from his mind; no matter, the pages were simply pages, written in dense English prose as prosaic as an accountant's end-of-year financial report.

Nevertheless, he dared not risk starting to read again. Another episode of whatever it was that had befallen him might be triggered. He could not bring himself to read, nor could he break his routine and leave the library early. At the same time, he was much too overwhelmed, too upset, to think properly about his experience even though he realised that some of it was already receding from him. The image of the document and the memory of reading from it remained, but he no longer recognised the script nor recalled the meaning of the words that he had spoken. He had a vague sense that he had felt at peace within himself after he had read aloud, but he had no idea why.

One thing was now startlingly obvious to him: his accomplished, if tortuous, thought processes of the previous Sunday's visit to the park had been for nothing. He could not dismiss *this* incident as something intrinsic to his own mind or personality. He recognised that the carefully reasoned accommodation of his dream and his subsequent awareness of an ache in his chest had been nothing more than an exercise in sophistry; he had been deluding himself. Quickly, he checked to see if the ache had returned; to his surprise there were no signs of it. Rather than finding comfort in this, it troubled him even further. Where was it? What was it? With a supreme effort he forced his mind to stop thinking, pushing his rising panic deep down into his stomach. He compelled himself to sit still, absolutely still.

Neither reading nor daring to reflect, lest the experience return or something even worse befall him, he sat, staring into space until his unerring internal clock alerted him that it was time to leave, to take the bus back to his apartment. He recognised the tell-tale signs of the tension building within him once more as he glanced at his watch repeatedly during the bus ride. He wanted to hurry home, to break into a run, but he could not allow himself to rush the four-minute walk from the bus stop to his apartment building. He sought the haven of its ordered peace and calm and the opportunity it would give him to confront this new menace: to confront and neutralise it. This time he would not allow himself to play any mind games: he would engage in hard research until he had eliminated all uncertainty. He would beat this, subjugate it, neutralise it.

Once inside his apartment, however, all resolve left him. He felt his strength drain from his body as if a valve has been opened. He didn't try to fight it; he let himself fall to the floor, unable to move. All thoughts of going to his laptop fled from his mind. His legs would take him no further and after a brief interval he stopped willing them to move. There was no point; his body had taken over, refusing to obey his mind. His mind began to shrink into itself until it attained a single point of focus, a single spot of relative calm. He caught it and held on to it; it became his world.

There he lay as the light outside dimmed, darkened as night fell and brightened again with the dawn. He lay without thought, without sleep, without awareness of his surroundings. Only with the rising sun, did he stir, his body clock knowing instinctively that it was 6am.

Automatically, he showered, dressed and breakfasted. Automatically, he walked to the bus stop and automatically, he found himself in the park that he had left only one week before in such heartened circumstances. Automatically, he began his cycles of walking and sitting, eating and drinking. Automatically, he returned again to his apartment. All the while, as his brain performed the necessary functions to keep his weekly routine on track, his mind held stubbornly to its internal focal point. Time stood still even as the day progressed around him.

As he closed the apartment door behind him he snapped immediately and unexpectedly back to his normal state of consciousness.

Though not quite normal, he quickly realised: a

sound that he could never recall making before emerged from his mouth: he began to laugh. Not only to laugh, but to laugh helplessly, uproariously. He laughed until tears streamed down his cheeks, until he had to fall to his hands and knees and crawl to his armchair, where he laughed until he felt that he was in danger of not being able to breathe. His ribcage hurt, his throat burned and still he laughed until, eventually, he slumped exhausted in his chair.

He was suddenly hungry, ravenously hungry. In his semi-catatonic state, he had managed to make sandwiches and bring coffee to the park; these he had consumed without paying attention to them, but now he wanted food, real food. He wanted to taste food, to savour it; he realised that he wanted to enjoy eating. Curiously, this did not surprise him, it seemed to be the most natural thing in the world even though he could not remember ever having had this craving before. He went to his freezer and from there to his kitchen. On Sunday evenings he always cooked himself a steak; for the first time in his life, he actively enjoyed eating it. With it, he drank his customary two glasses of wine, fine wine that he selected each week from a store near his work. He savoured it, sniffing it slowly and deeply, inhaling its aroma before sipping it and swirling it around his mouth. He did not drink enough to get intoxicated, but if he had he would not have noticed or cared.

All the time, the deepest sense of order, peace and calm that he had ever experienced continued to rest deep within him. More than that, it kept streaming to the surface, enveloping his mind and flooding his emotions. He didn't quite know what to do with himself; he had no idea that such a profound sense of peace could also be so exhilarating. It seemed a contradiction to the rational voice that rumbled in the background of his mind that peace could be exciting, but rationally or not, there he was, enjoying it. He knew intuitively that he had arrived somewhere important, more than that, somewhere *essential* and that he never wanted to be anywhere else or feel any other way ever again. Acknowledging his own sense of melodrama, he told himself in a mock-grandiose voice that he had found life. He smirked at the little piece of theatre that he had enacted; this too was a novelty.

He was aware that such a heightened sense of wellbeing was unlikely to remain forever; his rational mind had not absented itself and it offered this observation as a counter-balance to the near-euphoria that he felt. Even this realisation did not upset him. It was enough that he had attained something so distinctively new and positive; if necessary, he could either live on the memory or, perhaps, even seek it out again. Unlike his ruminations of a week earlier in the park, he was aware that he was not entirely making sense even to himself, but that too did not dampen his mood.

Eventually, his mood did subside, not to be replaced by the old sense of careful, studied neutrality, on guard every moment ready to protect itself, but by a settled calm. He found himself in a place that he could only describe as being blissfully benign… or was it benignly blissful? He smiled at his little witticism. He allowed himself to enjoy the moment.

In witness to this changed outlook, while he actively wanted to know why he felt this way, uncharacteristically, he did so, not fearfully, but expectantly, not out of compulsion, but out of genuine, personal interest. Yet another new experience presented itself: he found himself *interesting*.

As he considered his position he recognised that prior to his outburst of uncontainable laughter, his mind was something of a blank. He understood that it was Sunday evening, but he had difficulty in remembering anything since he had left his work the previous Friday afternoon. Slowly, without any sense of worry or panic, he began to trace his steps forward from the moment he left to get the bus back to his apartment after work. Longhorne always spoke and thought of the place he lived as 'his apartment', never as 'home'. Now he framed his memory search in revised terms: what could he remember from the time that he began his journey *home* after work? He smiled at the change in language and smiled again at the underlying change in him that it reflected.

He pressed his way carefully through the mists in his mind as if he were an explorer entering new lands until he was able to recall in outline the normality of his Friday evening and his journey to the library on Saturday morning. He got as far as the library doors and nothing further would come to him; his mind was a complete blank. He tried going in the opposite direction. He began with his memory of closing the door of his home behind him just before he gave way to his spasms of laughter, though he had no idea why, or if, that memory was significant. Bit by bit, he gained a sense of having been in the park. He wondered if this was really a memory of the day or simply an acknowledgement of how he had spent every Sunday for a decade, but he was reasonably certain that the memory was a true one. He recalled it as if he were looking through opaque glass, almost as if the memory was of someone else, but he recalled it nonetheless. He pushed himself to think harder, deeper, but the memories and images became increasingly vague; his efforts finally ran into the sand as he rewound his mind to 6am that morning.

He had, he mused, a missing day for which he had to account; to be precise a missing twenty-one hours. He smiled yet again, amused that the imperative he felt to count everything had clearly not deserted him. He toyed with his mind, trying to play tricks on it to see if he could catch it off guard, to cause it to offer up its hidden information. He began to read a book that he snatched at random from the nearest bookcase then flipped quickly to thinking of the missing day, *trying* to catch his mind off guard: nothing was forthcoming. He turned his armchair round, looked out the window at the evening sky, letting his mind wander with the gently moving clouds, allowing them to lull him almost to the point of dozing; still nothing came to him. He relaxed his eyes, permitting them to go out of focus as he stared at a fixed point on the wall beside the window, he willed his mind go blank: yet again nothing.

Remarkably, he was not upset at these failures. He felt no compulsion rising within him; none of the old familiar panic began to stir. He could *remember* how the compulsion and panic had felt, but he could no longer feel them as a present reality. They were like the memory of a pain that had long since passed; an injury that had long since been healed, leaving only a light scar to remind him of what once had been. As he thought of this, he became aware once more of the dull ache in his chest. It had returned, but he now experienced it as something other than an aching sensation. It was no longer like a weight attached to his heart though it still exerted pressure on him. It was as if something was swelling within his chest, not unpleasantly, but insistently nonetheless. He was right, he thought, to have identified this as signifying something that had always been there, but now he thought that whatever this was, it had been with him only in its most embryonic form for most of his life. The dream, the details of which he could still recall, had indeed alerted him to its presence also, but it had resided within him as a poor, starved version of whatever it was now becoming. It had begun to grow, to be nurtured, to become more fully part of him. Curiously, he reflected, perhaps he was becoming more fully part of it. The thought caused him no alarm, no disquiet; if anything, it seemed to deepen the sense of peace and calm that he felt.

It was, he thought, time to take stock. He noticed that time had slipped by and that he ought to be heading to his bedroom to sleep, but he shook off the thought. Although he had not slept for two days he did not feel tired and he did not feel any need to follow his established routine. Once again, he noted this, not with detachment, but with slight amusement: how peculiar, how quaint, his routines and habits seemed to him now. Instead of going to his bedroom, he made his way to the kitchen and poured himself a cup of strong coffee. He was pleased that he had always bought good-quality consumables even though he had taken little pleasure in eating or drinking them. He was pleased too that his apartment was furnished comfortably, though he baulked a little at the ubiquitous magnolia: that, he decided, he had to change.

As he sat down again, he felt that his previous, routine life, the life that he had lived for a decade, was like something that he had inherited. It was *his* life, but it seemed to him that he was not the person who had lived it. No, that was not quite right, he debated with himself. The person who had gone to the library and the person who had just finished enjoying steak and wine were versions of the same person, but they were very different versions. With the exception of 'the missing day', as he now chose to name it, he could recall his previous life as far back as his early adulthood, perhaps even a little into his adolescence, where his memories faded sharply, leaving his childhood a blank. The decade that he had lived in his apartment, he could remember with ease, although he acknowledged that there was not really much to remember.

How could he have been satisfied with that life? He thought of his life with a degree of sadness though felt no temptation to lapse into self-pity. Already he was beginning to think of 'his old self', accepting both continuity and discontinuity between himself as he now was and himself as he used to be. He knew that he ought to find this troubling, but instead he found it natural. He was what he now was; he had been what he once had been. He did not know what had caused the change, but abrupt and seemingly comprehensive as it was, he was entirely comfortable that the change had occurred and that he had emerged to be the new him. The thoughts tumbled through his head. Aware, that he wanted greater precision though didn't feel that he *needed* it, he forced himself to think calmly and began again, walking through his analysis step by step.

He felt that there was only one Longhorne, but that there were at least three iterations of him. There was the one he was now experiencing and that one he liked a lot. There was the one that had lived in this apartment for a decade whom he now viewed as having lived a shadow life. Then there was the pre-apartment Longhorne about whom he had thought very little over the years and about whom he knew virtually nothing, could remember virtually nothing. The new him was fascinated by his transformation and equally fascinated by his ability to analyse the span of his life as he was now doing; not 'researching' it as he might have done before, but rather opening himself fully to it. He did not want to deny his previous selves, although he did not feel a full connection with them. The change between the Longhorne who had left work the previous Friday and his current self, had been sudden, with entirely new attitudes and appetites appearing as if from nowhere. Well, surely not from nowhere, he reasoned; they must have come from within, from the feeling within his chest. Much of his old way of thinking also remained, however. He was able to reason, to analyse and to remember his pre-library life quite clearly. He was and was not the same person. He was satisfied with this thought.

His mind now concentrated on who and what he was before he had moved to his magnolia apartment. He accepted that he could not remember much about that version of himself. He noted the presence and importance of the twelve people to whom he had sent messages on each of his last ten birthdays. He knew why he did this, but he did not know precisely why the circumstances had arisen that made this annual gesture an essential part of whom he had been. Unlike 'the missing day', however, he felt that if he approached it correctly, he would be able to gain access to that part of his life. He would have to be careful, he must not force it, he reasoned; that would only make things more difficult and they were likely to prove difficult enough. He had to learn from his earlier, unsuccessful efforts. No amount of trying to *make* himself remember would result in a breakthrough. He would, he concluded, have to make his adolescent and childhood self the subject of enquiry, beginning in the morning.

Throughout this, Longhorne had no memory of his strange experience in the library, no memory of the foreign document or of reading aloud in a foreign language; no memory even of Andreas Palaiologos. He was curious about what had caused his transformation and he believed that whatever it was, it must have occurred during the missing twenty-one hours of this seminal weekend, but of the experience itself he had no recollection. He knew that it was related to the now pleasurable, essential feeling in his chest and that it was fundamentally connected to the internal order, calm and peace that had become an intrinsic part of whom and what he now was. What the cause of all this was, however, he was at a loss to identify and unless the missing hours came back to him, he recognised that it was likely to remain that way.

He could not explain to himself why this did not upset him. He was intrigued by the missing day, but it did not dominate his thinking and he certainly felt no compulsion to delve further into it. He had come to terms with his inability to remember those missing hours and concluded that, perhaps, that was the way things were meant to be. He relished his new peace that appeared to come organically from within and was happy that this gift had been given to him. Precisely because it was coming from within him, from the renewed feeling in his chest that wanted to grow and expand, he knew that it was there to stay; it was the new him.

The desire to find out about his early life, too, was not a compulsion, but an interest: a personal rather than an academic interest, but an *interest* nonetheless. He wanted to know what it was that had led to the apartment-dwelling Longhorne to live as he had done. He knew that there had to be some reason for him to have settled for such a twilight existence, inhabiting the leftovers of life. This intrigued him, but again it caused him no disquiet. Whatever his life had been, he wanted to find out about it because it seemed like the natural thing for his new self to do. It would have to wait for the morning, however, he realised as he began to feel agreeably sleepy.

He stretched and yawned in a satisfied way, noting that the clock in the kitchen informed him that it was almost midnight. His eye rested on the opened wine bottle on his dining table. Invariably, he poured the remainder of the bottle down the sink after his customary two glasses, but he had been so occupied with his thoughts that he had neglected to perform this duty. With a shrug, he poured himself a third glass before disposing of the bottle. He drank it slowly, appreciatively before washing up and retiring for the night, accepting happily that it was much too late to take his evening shower. He slept like a baby.

Five

Monday morning, the first weekday of Longhorne's enforced vacation: 6am came and went and he found himself still in bed. He was awake, but he had not stirred, feeling no inner imperative to get up, shower and follow his usual morning routine. On any other vacation, he would be preparing to spend the day in the library, but today he had decided to begin researching his past; his laptop beckoned.

Already, he had divided his life into three parts, three versions of himself. There was the present Longhorne, the 'magnolia' Longhorne of the past decade and the unknown Longhorne whose existence pre-dated the other two, but about whom he knew virtually nothing. Gaining knowledge of that version of himself was, he believed, critical to his understanding of both other versions of himself. He liked referring to his immediate predecessor as his 'magnolia self', but he was not satisfied at relegating the earliest version of himself to the category of 'unknown'. He settled on the term 'embryonic'. Today, he would begin to discover who and what the embryonic version of himself had been.

At 7am, he swung his feet out of bed, compelled the rest of his body to follow and headed for the shower. By 8am he had breakfasted. He felt a little uneasy that he was not on his way to the library, but he was determined not to give way to his old routines: routines that now seemed to him not only to be redundant, but ridiculously restrictive. Not for the first, and not for the last time, he pondered how he could ever have lived as he had for a decade. How could he have been so unaware of everything, so careless of the incidentals of life? His morning coffee tasted as never before, his cereal and toast constituted a banquet compared to the dull fuelling of his body that had habitually formed part of his morning ritual. The coffee and food were the same as always. He knew and understood that, just as he knew and understood that while they had not changed, he had.

Before he settled down to discover the embryonic Longhorne, he took time to look around his apartment. He liked most of what he saw. The furnishings were good, the apartment was clean and tidy, and the cupboards, fridge and freezer were well stocked with high-quality food. He wondered a little that he had such good taste when he had not taken any pleasure in eating or drinking, but mostly he was just glad that such had been the case. The only blot was the ubiquitous magnolia. He made a mental note, that regardless of his research, he was going to make time to go into the city and buy paint and brushes to transform his home. Pastel shades, he thought, would be pleasant: colourful, yet peaceful. If nothing else, by the end of his week off work, his apartment would no longer resemble a monastery. He smiled at the thought; he smiled again at the thought that he was getting used to smiling and then he smiled, just for the sake of smiling.

He decided that his dress code, too, would have to change. He resembled too much a budget airline flight attendant. He wasn't certain what dress code or style he ought to adopt, but he was certain that he could go beyond navy, white and black. In token that the magnolia Longhorne no longer ruled in his home, he removed the tie that he had unthinkingly knotted around his neck and sat at his laptop, open-collared. He felt a little thrill at the act of self-rebellion.

There was much work to be done, however, and he needed to crack on with it. He did so cheerily and expectantly, not knowing what he might find, but undaunted by the prospect he poured another cup of coffee and opened his laptop. Taking a deep breath, he typed in his own name in the search bar, more out of curiosity than any expectation that any results would appear. As anticipated, the only entries referred to other bearers of the Longhorne surname and there were not very many of them. Perhaps, he mused, that might change. He was a little startled at the thought even as it crossed his mind. He might be a new, reborn version of himself, but he still did not have any desire to become known to others, never mind to find, at some point in the future, a reference to himself on the internet. His new-found emancipation extended only as far as his own knowledge of his own life; knowledge of other people and their lives remained closed to him and knowledge of him would remain closed to them. He pushed the thought to the back of his mind, mildly irritated that it had appeared at all. He was determined, however, that nothing was going to spoil his mood; he continued with his research.

He quickly realised that the internet had no information to offer and no secrets to disclose. His online activity had been little more than a vestige of the magnolia Longhorne's way of thinking and operating; some old habits, it seemed, died hard. The new Longhorne knew that it was highly unlikely that he would find any trace of his name anywhere in the public domain. He knew this, *he was certain of it*, for reasons that he had not permitted himself to think about for years; not since he had moved into his present apartment.

He also knew in his heart that his calm acceptance the evening before of a missing day in his life was not simply the result of his unexpected and new-found lightness of spirit. There was a deeper reason why he had not reacted strongly to it. He knew, of course, that much more than a day of his life was missing from his memory; that much he had admitted to himself the evening before; that, after all, was the reason for his present research. Now, as he pushed the magnolia Longhorne further into the background he acknowledged that his memory was purposefully clouded; so purposefully clouded that he did not know if he could unveil what lay behind the barrier that he had, himself, constructed.

He was, nonetheless, committed to the task; he began to probe into his memories of his past, gently, but steadily. He could remember clearly the events immediately prior to moving in to his apartment, just after his twenty-first birthday. He knew that, at one time, he had also been able to recall much of the three or so years before that, but he had steadfastly refused to do so for the better part of a decade. A psychological sentry stood guard to those years, barring entry ruthlessly and effectively. Beyond that, the memories became increasingly vague until they ran out altogether in his adolescence. Of his childhood, he had no memory at all.

He was aware, too, of the reasons the magnolia Longhorne had crafted to prohibit himself from dwelling on his past; any reflection on it would have shattered his peace of mind instantly. After a few years of rigidly refusing to allow memories to come to the surface, he had become incapable of returning to his past and he found that it had no longer tried to force its way into his conscious mind. After a further few years, he had convinced himself that it had stopped even affecting his subconscious mind. Now he accepted that this was probably not so; he could not escape his past as he had once intended. More than that, he no longer wanted such to be the case.

He recognised that just a few days previously all of this had been a closed book to him; one that he had slammed shut with no intention of ever opening again.

So effectively had he forbidden his mind from returning to his past and so effective had been his chosen amnesia that he had truly ceased to think about it at all. He had lived as if the magnolia Longhorne had sprung into existence, wholly formed, at the age of twenty-one with his character, lifestyle, attitudes and aptitudes already fixed. With the exception of his annual card-mailing ritual, he had acknowledged no links to his past. Even there, his acknowledgement was confined to a stylised statement of closure, of separation from what had gone before. As the years had gone by, the ritual became something that he knew he had to perform to keep his sanitised world intact, but he had effectively forgotten why that was so. Now, the veil was being lifted from his eyes and he knew that his life of hiding in the shadows, of being entombed by his denial of his past, had to come to an end.

He marvelled a little at his own courage, at his willingness to open himself to the very things that he had tried so hard to suppress and yet he was eager to tackle them head-on. He felt calm, with just an undercurrent of energy bubbling beneath the surface. He knew that the Longhorne that he was about to discover was not quite him, but that it would help him to understand who he now was. At least, that was his hope.

Leaving the table and his laptop, he sat once more in his armchair. Symbolically, he had kept it turned to face the window from the evening before and for the first time in a decade he lifted the shutters in his mind. He had expected them to creak slowly open, but they rolled up smoothly as if they had closed only yesterday. Once open, the memories flowed easily, steadily and, to his surprise, painlessly.

He permitted himself to think of the hospital… of both hospitals. The burns unit came to mind first. He could recall the pain, the smell, the bandages, the dread that he felt each morning as he was woken at 6am prior to his bandages being changed and his wounds being cleansed. The burns had covered almost all of his back and ran from just below his shoulder blades to halfway down his calves. They had burned deeply into his flesh; third-degree burns in many places. They had taken months to heal, for the most part without the benefit of skin grafts: there simply wasn't enough skin on the rest of his body to utilise. Slowly, eventually the pain had subsided, the smell of burnt, then necrotic flesh gave way to the antiseptic scent of the single-bed unit that had been his home since his eighteenth birthday. He had emerged from the unit with the back of his body deeply scarred, but with his face and hair untouched. Sitting in his hospital chair, no one could have told that he had been injured at all.

In the months that it had taken him to recover, he recalled that no one had visited him. A first, he had not cared; his pain had been everything, blotting out all else. Then, as he had begun to recover, he assumed that visitors had been kept away because of the fear of infection. In the end no one ever came.

He could remember quite clearly being transferred from the burns unit to a psychiatric hospital, both of which were located in a city, thirty miles from the small town close to where he had then lived in the countryside. They were at the other end of the country from his present apartment; purposefully so. The psychiatric hospital was to become his home for almost two and a half years until his trial had been completed and he had been acquitted of all charges.

The trial he also remembered well. It had lasted only three weeks, but it had been delayed, first because of his physical injuries and then by a succession of psychiatric tests that had to be conducted before he was deemed fit to stand trial. His legal team that had been assigned his case through the legal-aid system had acted towards him in a perfunctory manner, doing their duty, but never going beyond what they deemed to be strictly necessary. He knew that his monosyllabic responses to their questions could not have helped, just as he knew that his uncooperative attitude had contributed to the tardiness of the psychiatric reports that eventually had concluded that he had not been suffering from any identifiable mental illness. The psychiatrists and psychologists had also stopped short of attributing any personality disorder to him, declining to state anything other than the obvious: he was excessively introverted. Had they been more successful in eliciting answers from him, they might have identified the scale of his disconnection with others, but they had dismissed his reticence to engage with others as a probable result of the trauma he had faced during and after the fire that had destroyed his home.

Not only his home, he reflected, but his family as well. Both his adoptive parents had perished in the fire that had consumed the old farmhouse in which he and they had lived. He had no siblings, at least none that he knew of, and he had no idea who his natural parents were. The fire, he was informed by police officers, had begun in the kitchen of the family home and had spread rapidly through the three floors of the rambling old house, searing through the attic bedroom that was his, before bursting through the roof. His parents had been asleep in their bedroom immediately above the kitchen and had died soon after the fire had taken hold. All of this, Longhorne had already known, but he listened to them as if they were imparting fresh information.

Longhorne had been found by the emergency services that had rushed to the scene, having been alerted to the blaze by neighbours who had seen the night sky lit up by the furnace. The nearest neighbours lived half a mile away, so there had been no hope of extinguishing the blaze or rescuing his parents by the time the fire crews arrived.

On their arrival, they had found Longhorne, in the early hours of his eighteenth birthday, sitting on the lawn in front of the house with his back turned to it, his clothes burned from his body. His memories of this were hazy and he was unclear now which were true memories and which were based on later comments by police or hospital staff. He did not speak to them as they wrapped him in their space blankets and he did not speak to the emergency-room hospital staff as they sedated him and began to work on his burns.

He did not speak to anyone very much until the detectives arrived at his single room in the secure unit of the psychiatric hospital. Then, as always, he spoke only in response to direct questions, saying the minimum required.

The psychiatric tests, he could remember quite clearly as well; increasingly clearly, as he allowed himself to dwell on that part of his life. The cognitive tests were simple, childishly so; the counselling sessions he had found inane and the counsellors' reports had offered little to his assessors. In the end he was charged with arson and murder. At the trial, in spite of his lawyers' misgivings, he had not taken the stand, but his judgement had been rewarded: there was insufficient evidence to convict him. He had gained notoriety for a time, but this was of no interest to him save that he found it necessary to relocate to a different part of the country, to assume a new name and lose himself in a large city, finding an undemanding desk job in an anonymous corporation. The world moved on and he had moved into what he now understood to be a further phase in his life. Strange, that what had once seemed to be his permanent self, his *only* self, he now viewed as a passing phase. He felt the distance between himself and his magnolia predecessor widen.

Longhorne quickly reassessed his categorisation: there were, it seemed, four, not three iterations of himself. Between his embryonic self and his magnolia self, there was the fire version of himself. He decided that before attempting to go further back, he would have to dwell a little longer on his fire-self.

That he was able and willing to do so, he knew ought to have taken him by surprise, but it didn't. Whoever or whatever he now was, or was becoming, he seemed to have an unresistingly open mind, eager to explore and to face whatever was there to be discovered.

He smiled again; so be it.

Six

He *had* started the fire; not as an act of arson, but as an act of carelessness. He *was* responsible for his adoptive parents' death, but he had not murdered them.

He had been sitting alone in the farmhouse kitchen after midnight. His parents had gone to bed, as was their custom, at 10pm. Longhorne usually retired to his own room at the top of the old building shortly after, but on this occasion, he wanted to be awake as his eighteenth birthday was chimed in by the grandfather clock in the hall. He was not in the least dismayed that he was alone; he knew that his parents would greet him with birthday wishes in the morning and that there would be a quiet family meal in the evening during which presents and cards would be dutifully offered and dutifully received.

He had listened to the radio for an hour after his parents had retired; he recalled the discussion well: a debate on the rights and wrongs of euthanasia. As with most such debates, the participants had held rigidly to their views, their opinions cancelling each other out as they argued over the same statistics, the same examples, the same evidence. He had listened avidly as he always did to in-depth radio discussions, but at the end of it he was unable to form a clear opinion on the subject. Whether inherited from his natural parents or developed through contact with his adoptive father, Longhorne had a pathological inability not to see all sides of an argument; coming to a settled mind on any given topic was a virtual impossibility for him.

Having turned the radio off, he had sat thinking about the discussion. His mind turned away from the topic of euthanasia to thoughts of dying and from there to thoughts of suicide. As he reflected, now, in his magnolia apartment, he was aware that the turn in his thoughts then was not as melodramatic as it now seemed. He had not been thrust into suicidal thoughts by the radio discussion; he had simply let his mind drift, idly at first, in that direction. He could not now recall if he had harboured such thoughts before, but he remembered that as midnight and his eighteenth birthday approached, the thought of drifting off into an everlasting dreamland had seemed the most attractive prospect in the world. Perhaps that had been a recurring thought in his adolescence, surely it could not have struck him for the first time just before his eighteenth birthday, but he would have to leave that investigation until later, when he would try to get in touch with his earlier 'embryonic' self.

On the stroke of midnight, heralded by the familiar and usually comforting chimes of the grandfather clock, he permitted himself a truly melodramatic moment, he wished himself a happy birthday and turned on the gas oven, just as he had done on many late evenings to boil milk for a bedtime drink. This time, he didn't light the flame; he was determined to let the gas flow until it sent him to sleep and into the welcome dreamworld that awaited him. He lay down on the old sofa that stood at the back of the kitchen and began to order his thoughts; not reflecting on his life, but on the dreams that he wanted to inhabit his mind as it drifted from his body into an eternal sleep. This was the most natural thing in the world: why had he not done it sooner? To be free to inhabit his own world at will; how could he refuse to enter through the portal that beckoned him?

He could feel his mind becoming foggy, however, as sleep begin to creep towards him. He found it increasingly difficult to concentrate, to order his thoughts. The world of his own creation blurred in his mind, it fractured, reformed itself, but not in the way that he wanted. Suddenly, panic stuck him: what if this was a foretaste of what was to come and he could not order his dreams as he wished in his everlasting sleep? What if they became nightmarish? What if he did not dream at all?

With an effort, he flung himself off the sofa and staggered towards the kitchen door, into the darkened corridor that led to the hallway that separated him from the front door of the farmhouse. The smell of gas followed him; he stumbled against the furniture that cluttered the corridor; his parents had always been hoarders of bric-a-brac and antiques. Without thinking, he reached out to find the light switch beside the front door and flipped it on. The ancient wiring sparked as it always did. His world exploded.

The fireball seared his back. Instinctively he had hunched as the flames flashed around him. He turned the handle of the front door, unlocked as always in its rural security, and threw himself into the darkness. He tore off his burnt clothes, staggered forward until he was clear of the burning house and sat in the driveway, not knowing what else to do. He could feel the conflagration on his back, he could hear the crack of burning timbers; he was unaware of the screams coming from his parents' bedroom. Within minutes it was over; the dry wooden ceilings and beams of the farmhouse, the cluttered furniture, the wooden panelling on the stairs had made an ideal bonfire. The flames soared high into the sky, alerting neighbours. The emergency services arrived and he was hurried to hospital. He remembered being asked if there was anyone else in the house; he recalled saying nothing in response to the fire crew. What would have been the point? His parents could not have survived beyond the first few minutes, perhaps even less. Even as he was rushed to the ambulance, he remembered reading once that most fire victims succumbed to smoke inhalation rather than to the flames. He noted the thought, dispassionately, before the pain began to hit, before it took over everything else. As he arrived at the hospital and the emergency-room staff sedated him his final, conscious thought was that perhaps he was dead after all and this was a nightmare from which he would never waken.

He had lain sedated for two weeks before he was brought out of his induced coma. His life was no longer in danger, but months of pain, surgery and isolation lay ahead. The hospital staff kept their distance from him. The doctors and nurses were correct with him, doing their duty with professional competence, but they never engaged him in anything other than necessary, clinical conversation. A chaplain had called to see him, but he left and did not return after he had been met with a wall of silence. Longhorne had never been particularly communicative, but now he was silent almost all the time. He spoke only when spoken to or when, as his recovery continued, he asked someone to order a new book for him to read. To try to keep his mind off the pain and the tedium of the hospital routine, he began to read voraciously, lying on his stomach while the wounds on his back healed. The first book that he had picked up was a volume on the history of the Roman Empire; thereafter he read only history books.

Sitting now in his apartment armchair, he could remember how he had felt: alone, vulnerable, in need of comfort, but unable to ask for it, knowing that even if it had been offered he would not have known how to receive it. Instead, he gritted his teeth during the morning dressing of his wounds and kept them firmly closed throughout the rest of the day. He understood that his parents had died, but he was surprised, at first, that the few members of his extended family known to him (his father's sister and her husband) had failed to visit him. They had not been close to him, or he to them and he imagined that they would have had little to say to one another, but he had expected them to exercise some form of familial duty.

After a few weeks, the realisation dawned that they had not come to see him because they associated him with his parents' deaths; his aunt must have believed that he had been responsible in some way for the fatal fire, responsible for her brother and his wife's lives coming to an end, and she resented him for it. He vaguely remembered her husband as a docile, compliant soul; when his wife spoke, he invariably agreed. Still, a call to see how he was recovering, physically and mentally, was the least he had expected. Slowly, he realised that their absence stemmed from a more sinister motive. Once the hospital staff had told him that the police wanted to interview him when he was sufficiently recovered, his suspicions were confirmed; they not only thought that he was responsible for the fire that killed his parents, they suspected that he had started it deliberately.

When he had absorbed this, he was glad that they hadn't come; he wouldn't have known how to respond to their comments or questions. Worse still, in his awkwardness, he might have said something that they would have interpreted as confirming their suspicions. He was grateful that the staff had alerted him to the police's intentions; they had given him ample time to think and to plan. It seemed that the detectives were not going to attempt to speak to him until he had been discharged from the burns unit and it soon became apparent to him that a decision had been made to admit him to a psychiatric hospital. He had not been consulted about this; initially the nurses had simply made vague pronouncements that he would continue his recovery 'elsewhere'. He did not question them; he did not really care where he went next. Nevertheless, it came as something of a shock to him to discover that he had been 'sectioned' and that he would not be released until others were satisfied of his sanity and their safety.

He rapidly determined that maintaining silence was his best course of action, though he knew that once he had been transferred he would have to cooperate sufficiently in order not to be diagnosed as being mentally ill. He had not particularly cared where his recovery was to be completed, but he had no desire to spend longer in a psychiatric hospital than was necessary. First though, even as he lay recovering from its effects, he knew that he had to recall the night of the fire; he had to assess his own actions and motives as clearly and as honestly as he was able.

Had he really considered suicide or somehow, subconsciously had he wanted to destroy his home or even hurt his parents? He had ample time to mull over the questions in his mind. He found it difficult to see why he had entertained the thought of ending his life and wondered at the strange thought processes that had led him to think that he would have spent an eternity in an everlasting dreamworld. He had not been religious, nor had he harboured any real convictions about the possibility of an 'after-life' (he had been unable to decide), yet he knew that his mind had drifted sincerely, if foolishly, in that direction, leading him to take the fateful course of action on the cusp of his eighteenth birthday. He was glad that he had snapped out of his stupor before he had succumbed to the gas fumes, but as he lay in his hospital bed he felt disconcerted at the events that had followed.

Disconcerted: he felt that was an accurate way to describe his feelings. He was not grief-stricken or appalled; he did not feel guilty or devastated by his parents' deaths. He had not needed the hospital staff to tell him that his parents had perished in the fire; that had been evident to him from the start, even as he sat on the grass in front of the house with his back to the blaze. When they did tell him, however, he was uncertain of his response: he had thought that confirmation of their deaths might have released a flood of emotion or that fond memories would start to tumble through his mind. Instead, he felt unease, a vague sense of loss, but nothing that he could identify as real sorrow, nothing that constituted mourning. He could not have anticipated that he was going to react in this way. Without thinking about it very much, he had always assumed that he had loved them just as he had assumed that they had loved him. His lack of emotional contact with them, with their deaths, surprised him, but he noted it as though he were an observer. Initially, he put his lack of reaction down to shock, then delayed shock, but the connection with them never surfaced, never returned; eventually he began to doubt that it had ever been there.

He told himself that the fire had been an accident, a stupid, unnecessary accident. He had warned his parents that the wiring in the house was ancient and ought to be replaced, but they were old and set in their ways. In a way, he reflected, the accident was as much their fault as it was his; if they had listened to him nothing terrible would have happened. On the night of his foolish dalliance with suicide, he could have merely stood outside the house, filled his lungs with clear air and returned to switch off the gas. Windows would have been opened and the air cleared; they would have known nothing about it the next morning and his birthday would have run its course as expected. Now, because of their obstinate refusal to effect repairs on the old farmhouse, they were dead. It was their own obstinacy that had led to their ruin.

As he thought along these lines in the weeks following the fire, he became more and more convinced that he was not solely responsible for their deaths; in fact he had little responsibility to bear at all. It was true that if he had boiled milk for his night-time drink as usual, instead of giving way to an inexplicable whim, he and they would probably be sitting now in the farmhouse kitchen, living their quiet lives as before. He was not to blame, however, for the curious suicidal thoughts that had captivated his mind, nor for the strange allure of the dreamworld that he had sought. Those things had simply come to him as if of their own volition; he had not commanded them nor conjured them deliberately from his own imagination. He certainly wasn't to blame for the faulty light switch or the decrepit wiring. Quite the contrary: they were to blame, they were responsible. He began to resent them: *they* had placed him in this position. They were the cause of his pain, they were the cause of the predicament he now found himself in. They no longer had to suffer, but he did. No wonder that he felt no emotions of sadness at their passing. Perhaps, he permitted his mind to whisper, they had deserved to die after all.

He was shocked at the thought even as it lodged itself in his mind. He was shocked then and even more so now as he sat in his apartment reviewing the thought processes of his past self. He was shocked, but he could not deny what he had thought. Looking out the window of his apartment, he was mildly surprised that he still wanted to continue with his investigation, but although he found the memory unsavoury, it did not diminish his desire to explore further his 'fire-self'. He was set on a pathway of self-discovery and even though he was unsure of the moral relationship between various iterations of himself, nothing was going to distract him from pursuing his goal, however unpleasant his findings might be. He even felt a little proud of himself, at his courage and integrity. He permitted himself a brief self-congratulatory moment before returning to his reflections.

Admitting that he harboured the thought that his adoptive parents had brought about their own demise and that, in some way, they deserved their fate had given him all the more reason to be quiet when the police came to interview him. They didn't come until a week after he had 'settled in' to his new surroundings. The staff at the psychiatric hospital were more forthcoming, more engaging than the staff at the burns unit. They had made something of an effort to be pleasant to him, to make him feel at home. *Home*: that was a term that he hadn't used of the old farmhouse; he had always referred to it in his mind as well as in speech as 'the farmhouse'. Strange that the hospital staff wanted him to feel 'at home'. It was a word he felt did not belong in his vocabulary any more than it had belonged in his experience.

The hospital was an old building, set in its own grounds behind high walls. In some ways it reminded him of the farmhouse, the same creaking floorboards, the same odd assortment of ill-matching furniture gathered piecemeal over the years. He conjured a little joke with himself: the hospital he referred to as the new farmhouse. He found this amusing though he couldn't quite say why. He was encouraged to take walks in the hospital grounds, to have his meals with other 'guests'. He was happy to do the former; the latter he accepted as a necessary part of appearing not to be mentally ill. He was not good company and soon he ate his meals first in silence at the end of a table, then at a table on his own and eventually he was permitted to take his meals on a tray either outside if the weather was fair or in his room. He was careful not to be rude or confrontational; merely reserved and self-isolated.

All the while, he continued to read voraciously, passing hours devouring history books. Once, a nurse had introduced a novel to him, setting it on his beside table in the sparsely furnished, single room that he occupied, but he had left it unopened. Trying again, she had brought a book written by a well-known travel writer thinking that this might spark his interest. It too, remained unopened. He did not comment or complain; he just ignored it. As with his meals, he soon got his way and the flow of history books resumed.

These were but small, easily won skirmishes in the conflict between him and the hospital staff. The real battles were to be fought over their attempts to gain access to his mind. For these he had developed a clear strategy and employed deliberate tactics. He knew that he had to surrender some ground: enough to enable them to decide whether or not he was fit to stand trial. It was essential, for his plan to succeed, that they believed they understood him well enough to declare that he was not mentally ill, but they must not be permitted to break down any of his real defences. They must not be allowed any insight into the true workings of his mind. In truth, he did not know what lay there, but there was always the possibility that something lived in the recesses of his brain that would be a matter of concern to them. If there was, *he* did not want to know about it, never mind wanting to grant *them* access to it. His thoughts were to remain private, accessible to him alone, and even then they were to be limited in scope and depth.

As with the generals in the history books that he had been reading, he understood that he needed to hone his plan, to fine-tune a strategy that would guide him through the many battles that he would have to fight. Without raising suspicions, he would ensure that a sufficient number of the history books he ordered would contain memoirs of great military and political figures. He would learn from them; learn how to give way here, to take ground there, so that he would emerge triumphant at the end of the war. He had to keep one step ahead of *them* at all times, never letting down his guard, never trusting anyone other than himself. He had to stay alert.

Seven

The psychiatrists that were responsible for his care were not at all happy that they had been forced into the role of being court servants, but they had no choice. It was a role that they were used to performing from time to time, but it was unwelcome nonetheless. In Longhorne's case they were initially troubled that the added legal burden would compromise his psychiatric care. They were prepared to accept that he had been 'sectioned' pending their assessment of whether or not he was likely to be a danger to himself or others, but they would have preferred to do this without the shadow of a criminal investigation hanging over them. In addition to whatever else they might discover, they expected to find a very disturbed young man, scarred mentally as well as physically by the fiery ordeal he had endured. Addressing the needs of their damaged patient ought to be their priority; indeed, it ought to be their only responsibility. Their court-mandated role, however, had tasked them with trying to discover the person that was there before the fire as well as assessing the current mental state of their patient. They had to provide the court with information that would enable it to decide whether Longhorne had been mentally competent on the night of the fire and also they had to determine whether he was mentally fit to stand trial. These issues were chief in the minds of the police and the prosecuting authorities; as far as they were concerned, other considerations could wait.

The police had become involved at a very early stage. The fire service had quickly established the source of the fire that had completely destroyed the old farmhouse. Sifting through the charred shell of the building, they had also discovered what remained of Longhorne's adoptive parents. Relying on dental records, they were able to make a positive identification within a matter of days. A routine enquiry into a domestic fire, turned into a murder investigation. In the absence of any other viable theory and in the face of Longhorne's silence, caused, at first, by the nature of his recovery from his injuries but maintained even after he was discharged from the burns unit, the police had concluded that he had started the fire. Given the location and the nature of its origin, they posited that his actions had been deliberate. They had interviewed him briefly just after his transfer from the burns unit to the psychiatric hospital, had gained nothing to add or subtract from their theory and had sought to press charges. It was agreed by all concerned that there was probably a case to answer, but any progress towards a formal arrest and potential trial was made subject to psychiatric assessment. In brief, the psychiatrists had to determine whether or not he was sane.

Once the worst of his physical recovery had passed, Longhorne had been able to give his attention to the dilemma he faced: on the one hand, he did not want to stand trial and risk being found guilty, but on the other he did not want to countenance the prospect of spending the rest of his life in a psychiatric hospital if he was deemed to be insane. He understood that the circumstantial evidence in his case suggested a poor outcome for him. After all, he *had* started the fire and he had made no attempt, however vain the effort might have been, to save his parents; he had not even told the fire fighters that they were in the house. The tale of his aborted suicide attempt, if that indeed was what it had been, seemed an uncertain foundation for a defence against a murder charge. It might, he reasoned, be accepted as part of a not-guilty plea, based on grounds of diminished responsibility, but that would mean that he would have to consent to being classified as being mentally ill; not only mentally ill, but dangerously so. His knowledge of the law was sketchy, but he concluded that his best option was to convince the psychiatrists that he was sane and so able to stand trial if charges were pressed, but at the trial to remain silent, feigning trauma from the extent of his injuries and the horror of the fire. He would impress upon the psychiatrists and the court that he simply could not face thinking about, never mind talking about, the fire and the death of his parents. He felt uncomfortable at adopting such tactics, but he assuaged his conscience by convincing himself that this was the only course of action that would result in him being treated fairly. He knew that he was innocent of murder, but he also knew that he faced an uphill struggle in persuading anyone else to agree with him.

Having determined this course of action while he was still in the burns unit waiting transfer to the psychiatric hospital, very quickly everyone became either an enemy or a threat and he approached them as such. The police, clearly, were his enemies and had to be fought at every step; the psychiatrists and even his own lawyers were threats who could expose him to danger. He trusted no one, cut himself off from any counsel offered and plotted his own course. He became increasingly insular, viewing everyone around him solely as means or obstacles to achieving his ends.

As he became more and more withdrawn, relying on his own fortitude alone, a new seed formed and began to take took root in his mind. He bemoaned his misfortune, focusing on his belief that his parents' deaths were the cause of all his trouble. Without their deaths, without their obstinacy and stupidity, without their inability to perform routine domestic repairs, there would be no threat to him, he would have no dilemma to face. It seemed a small and logical step to take: they too became his enemies. In his mind and, more importantly, in his conscience they were transformed from merely being responsible for their own deaths to becoming his opponents in his fight for survival. There was no going back: they were cut off completely from him and would remain so, had to remain so.

Reflecting on this in his apartment, he knew that not only had his reasoning been flawed, but that his moral compass had failed him: he had done his parents a disservice. In their way, they had loved him; he knew that. He also knew that in his own way, he had loved them. At least, he concluded that he must have loved them, but he could neither remember nor resurrect any real feelings towards them at all. If love meant appreciating their care of him and recognising his debt to them, he loved them. If it meant something more, he would have to assume that he loved them; it would have been unreasonable for him not to have.

He also recognised the extreme stress that he had been under and that he had been fighting for his survival: the choice between a life spent in prison or a life spent in a secure psychiatric unit was a choice of location only; the misery would have been the same to him. Easily, naturally Longhorne understood his 'fire-self', understood him and just as easily forgave him.

Determined to be honest with himself, Longhorne admitted that he not only understood his fire-self; he had a certain admiration for him. He could not but applaud the ingenuity his fire-self had shown in treading the careful path he had chosen. The various psychiatric tests he had passed with ease, showing no weakness in reasoning or any lack of awareness of his surroundings. He performed well in psychometric tests, easily giving the answers and making the responses he believed would demonstrate both that he was sane and that he did not suffer from any established personality disorder. During the counselling sessions that touched either on the circumstances of the fire or on his relationship with his parents, he remained silent, at best offering monosyllabic answers. At the first hint that a session was turning in that direction, he would exude palpable unease and then give the impression of shutting down mentally, drifting off to a 'safe place' in his mind. In reality he kept feverishly alert, watching the counsellors carefully as they observed him, noting each counsellor's distinctive expressions, learning not only how to interpret but also how to anticipate and then neutralise their tactics. His face was impassive, but inside he was a tangle of fear, craft and planning.

He wanted to know more about the legal process he was trapped in just as he wanted to understand better the psychological clues that his interrogators (for such he viewed them) were seeking to find, but he knew better than to order books on law or psychology or to make use of the unit's computers to look at online articles. He understood that all of this would be monitored and that he had to be constantly on guard not to give away the secrets of his deceit. He had to rely on a mixture of natural cunning and his well-developed intelligence. He was, he knew, walking at times in the dark, guessing at potential court processes as well as the ways in which his psychiatrists might be assessing him. For the greater part, he guessed right.

The process was slow, even painstaking. Tests had to be conducted, counselling courses completed and reports written. Second opinions had to be sought and at the end of it all, the prosecution had to determine whether or not they believed that there was a reasonable prospect of securing a conviction. Eventually, more than two years after the fire, he was assessed as having been mentally competent at the time of his parents' deaths, that he had a case to answer and that he should stand trial. Within a few months his case came before the court.

He was prepared to accept this slow process, to mark it down as a price worth paying to secure his long-term freedom. He was consumed by one thought alone: to emerge at the end of his purgatory, a free man. He liked the analogy: the fire had truly become his purgatory. It had cleansed him from the cares and attachments of his former life; he would not only survive it, he would be the better for it, refined by it. The fire, however much pain it had caused him physically and however much mental testing had come from it, had been a positive, even a good, thing. To it, and it alone, he owed his new start in life.

These thoughts, however, did not change his opinion of his parents; he refused to see them as playing any part in his redemption. They were part of the reason that he had to undergo purgation in the first place; they were part of what had to be purged from his life. Sitting in the armchair in his lounge, Longhorne could not recall quite how these thoughts had formed in his mind or why they had seemed so self-evidently right to him at the time. He understood that in fighting for his survival, he had not considered the degree of trauma that he had to absorb or the degree to which, in truth, he had become his own tormentor. Now, reflecting on it all more than a decade later, he began to see just how damaged he had been.

How, he pondered, could he have made such connections in his mind? How could he have reacted so violently against his parents, blaming them, in essence, for everything? Was it really that he had felt himself caught up in a desperate fight for survival or was there something deeper, more sinister behind the machinations of his mind? Again, he postponed his pursuit of the thought; better first to finish recounting the trial and its aftermath; then he would turn his attention to the pre-fire, the embryonic Longhorne. Perhaps then he would find more deeply hidden clues to the genesis of his character and personality.

The trial played out very much as he had hoped and planned. The psychiatrists had declared him sane, but emotionally damaged as a result of the fire and its aftermath. The damage was profound, but they did not believe him to be a danger to himself or to others. There was no reason, in their opinion, to keep him confined to a psychiatric hospital, although they advised strongly that he would benefit from further intensive counselling. The matter of his guilt or innocence, they left to the court.

His legal team, on their first meeting, had advised him to take the witness stand and give a full and open account of what had happened. They were soon at a loss to know how best to represent him: he refused to disclose even to them his memories of that night. In fact, he did not speak to them about it at all, feigning once more, trauma at the thought of having to cast his mind back to that terrible event. He would barely countenance a discussion about the impending trial, lest it cause him distress. In the end, they had no other recourse than to accept that he would remain silent during his trial. They had warned him that juries do not, as a rule, look kindly on defendants refusing to give evidence at their own trials, but they made the best of the hand they had been dealt. They emphasised to the jury that all the evidence against their client was entirely circumstantial. They drew attention to his own horrific physical injuries and they highlighted his emotional and psychological distress. Above all, they urged the jury not to convict unless they were certain, beyond reasonable doubt, that he had intended to murder his parents by fire.

The jury could not be certain; he was acquitted.

He did not feel elation at the verdict; he did not even really feel relief. Thinking back on it now as he sat in his armchair, Longhorne realised that he had felt nothing because he had then determined to remove all feeling, all emotion from his life. Feelings represented weakness, potential avenues for further trauma. He had endured enough distress from the fire and its aftermath, enough turmoil to last him a lifetime. Enough was enough, he had concluded. His life would henceforth be his and his alone; as far as he could, he would make it impervious to outside influences or disruptions. He would seek and he would find peace, order and calm, and nothing would ever again intrude into the sanctuary of his mind. He would allow only those things that helped secure his independence, his emotional isolation from the rest of the world, to enter his sphere. He would eat and drink, he would earn a living, he would read history books, but he would not engage, he would *never* again engage with others.

The fire was an instantly closed chapter in his life; his purgatory was over and the rest of his life could now begin. He would put his past behind him and with it any dependence on others. After all, had he not accepted the rules and regulations set by his parents, had he not thought it disrespectful to challenge them more firmly about the need to rewire the old farmhouse, his misery would have been avoided. In the future, he would live independently from everyone. He would allow himself no access to others and others no access to him. The past, he determined, would remain a closed book to him

He did, however, insist on one link to his past. As with many of his decisions, he was not sure where the thought originally came from or why he felt a compulsion to follow it through even though it ran counter to his new determination to begin an entirely new life, but it lodged in his mind and he decided to acquiesce to it. When his trial was concluded he conducted a little research project. He matched the names of the twelve people on his jury to addresses that he eventually managed to attribute to them. It took him a few weeks, but he was assured to his own satisfaction that he had got it right. On each of his subsequent birthdays, he sent them cards on which he wrote a single message: his age.

At the beginning, perhaps this was his way of thanking them symbolically for acquitting him and also a way to remind himself that had it not been for them, he would have spent each birthday in prison. Quickly, the meaning of the ritual changed to become his way of marking the definitive separation point between his old and his new lives at the end of his purgatory. As the years passed and he blotted out of his mind the details of the fire, his confinement in hospital and his trial, this annual routine simply became part of his ritualised life. It was a way of maintaining his requisite order and calm. He had no idea if his jurors still lived at the same addresses or even if they were still alive.

He didn't care.

Eight

The morning had taken its toll on Longhorne. He needed time to let the newly accessed memories settle in his mind before launching into the next part of his investigation. He intended to delve back beyond the fire to find out something about his adolescence and perhaps even his childhood. At the same time, he was delighted with what he had accomplished. To have flung back the curtain to expose the three years of his life that he had kept hidden under wraps for a decade was no mean feat.

He felt more than a little pleased with himself, but also surprised that he had not recoiled from the memories he had allowed to come flooding back. The experience had not been nearly as painful as he had expected; in fact, he realised that it hadn't been painful at all. He was more fascinated by his past than repelled by it. He also felt a little dissociated from it. In some ways, recovering those memories had been like watching a documentary about someone else's life rather than his own. Of course, he thought, that was, in a sense true: the experiences that he had recalled *were* the experiences of someone else: his fire-self.

At the same time, they didn't seem entirely like memories at all; the events seemed fresh, familiar, recent. It was as if the intervening decade had not happened and his trial and acquittal had taken place only a few weeks previously. He realised that he felt more in tune with the fire Longhorne than he did with the magnolia one. The last decade of his life, he began to view as a missing decade, one during which he had disappeared. And yet, he knew that wasn't quite true. The magnolia Longhorne *had* been a real, if narrow and restricted, version of himself while the new one was not quite the same as the fire version either. Perhaps the magnolia Longhorne was a necessary bridge from one to the other.

Perhaps; perhaps not… he stopped himself from musing further. In a quite pleasant way, Longhorne's head was buzzing, but he knew that this was a sign that he needed to switch off from his internal dialogue; he needed to clear his head before returning to his quest.

If the old Longhorne had ever done the unthinkable and had managed to quell his compulsion to keep drilling down until he had restored complete equilibrium to his life once more, at this point he might have considered reading a book from his extensive library to settle himself, but the new Longhorne realised that he was turning into something of a man of action. He looked again at the walls of his apartment and decided that it was time to decorate.

He had no idea what time the buses ran into town from outside his apartment other than when they enabled him to carry out his daily work commitments or weekly library routines. Having made himself a quick sandwich for lunch, he strolled to the stop and waited for the first bus to arrive. He noted that he had counted neither the number of steps he had taken nor the number of seconds he had spent walking. He knew the number of lamp-posts had not changed from the day before, but he had not bothered to check. He smiled; he found himself amusing.

The bus duly arrived and he made his way to a DIY store close to his workplace. He had to shop close to his workplace; this was the only route into town that he knew. Unsure of how much paint to buy or which brushes and rollers to purchase he engaged an assistant in conversation. Again, to his mild surprise he noted that he managed to engage her also in a little small talk. All of this came to him quite naturally. He was aware that he had not deliberately decided to be more sociable than usual (which, he acknowledged, would not have been difficult to achieve) nor had he determined to make an effort with the shop assistant; it just happened. Whoever or whatever his new version was, he was no more in control of it than he had been of the magnolia version. He was still partly detached from himself, able to observe his own thoughts, feelings and actions, all of which seemed to have a life and energy of their own. He believed, though he was not certain, that he could step in at any point and stop what they were doing, but he felt no desire to do so. The new him was much too interesting; too full of surprises. He wanted to see where *he* would take him.

He eventually settled on pastel shades of peach for his lounge, lavender for the bedrooms and, in a departure from his original intentions, a surprisingly zesty lemon for his hallway and bathroom. He felt a tinge of excitement at his purchases and hurried home (he used that word again) in time to get a first coat of paint on his lounge walls while the light was still good. All in all, as he stepped back and surveyed the freshly glistening walls, he felt more than satisfied with the day's accomplishments.

The day, however, was far from done. After a pleasant meal of pasta carbonara which he made from fresh ingredients, he settled back in his armchair to resume his search.

What came before the fateful night of the fire? *Fateful night*; a little melodramatic, he thought, though not inaccurate or inappropriate. It *had* changed his life completely, it had cut him off from the members of his wider family and, if course, it had brought his parents' lives to an end.

At that thought, he paused. Perhaps this was not yet the time to delve into his childhood and adolescence. Didn't he owe his late parents some further thought, perhaps a greater degree of respect? Didn't he owe himself some time to reflect on their lives, perhaps even some time to mourn?

He baulked a little at the idea, but felt compelled to pursue it further, partly from a sense of duty that imposed itself on his mind, but partly also from curiosity. As yet, there were no emotions involved that he could discern, no desire to remember his parents because he felt any great loss. He wasn't aware of any deep-seated sorrow that had been stirred up by the memories he had allowed back into his mind; perhaps that would come later.

He thought of them dispassionately as one might think of a book or a play that had to be reviewed as a matter of professional duty. He allowed his mind to conjure up their appearances, to see them in their natural habitat of the old farmhouse. He recalled the sound of their voices, the manner of their movements, their smell. He recalled also the atmosphere in the home: familiar, predictable, pleasant though undoubtedly dull. In his mind, the farmhouse and, in particular the kitchen, began to take on the aspect of a display cabinet, his parents caught in amber as if they were specimens of an extinct species on view. Changing the metaphor a little, he thought that he was observing them as one might observe one of the less popular exhibits in a zoo. He felt no unease at thinking of them in this way; it was the way it was.

His father had been a quiet, reserved man in his mid-sixties at the time of his death. He was bald, apart from wispy strands of grey hair at the sides and back of his head, had a heavy moustache and was small of stature. His build was neither athletic nor portly, but testament to a life lived in moderation; his voice soft and devoid of texture. He moved slowly, inexorably getting from one destination or task to another without fuss or any outward sign of enthusiasm.

He invariably wore a suit, even at weekends, and always had a tightly knotted tie complementing a white shirt which he always kept fully buttoned at the collar. Apart from work, he seldom left the house. He did not belong to any clubs that Longhorne was aware of and did not attend any sporting or other events that were not directly associated with fulfilling the social obligations of his job. When he had to attend such functions, he went with determined resignation; he went alone, he completed his duties and he returned home as quickly as was decently possible. Longhorne recognised that his father had been a walking caricature of the country solicitor that had been his chosen profession: not an avuncular, golf-club type of solicitor, but a musty desk-bound servant of a firm in which he had never harboured either desires or hopes of being made a partner. He specialised in conveyance and often spread property maps on the kitchen table as he pored over land boundaries, to be shooed gently out of the way, on occasion, by his wife as she prepared supper.

She was precisely the sort of woman that one might expect to be married to this quiet, unassuming man: small, birdlike with a chirping cheeriness that always threatened, but never quite managed to grate enough to invoke censure: consistently mildly annoying, but not offensive. Like her husband, Longhorne could not recall her ever raising her voice or displaying anger or even displeasure. She took no interest, it seemed to him, in the world beyond the farmhouse, her family and small circle of female friends that she met once a week in the nearby town for tea, scones and... and? Longhorne realised that he had no idea what she and her friends might have talked about. As far as he could remember (and he *would* press his memory further on this, he determined) she took no interest in the news bulletins and current-affairs programmes that his father listened to on the kitchen radio and she never offered an opinion during the sporadic discussions that he and his father would have.

His parents lived in a social and domestic no-man's-land: in a state that fell short of genuine contentment, but which lacked enough passion to evoke discontent. They seemed accustomed to one another, to their lot in life and to their routines and rituals. They were undemanding, unexceptional and undeveloped; they lacked contours or colour.

Had Longhorne considered writing a novel, he reflected, he would have made the tragic victims of a domestic fire much less predictable, much less *magnolia* than his parents had been. Even his newly stirring imagination, hitherto unused to much exercise, could have invented more interesting characters than his parents had been in real life.

Even as the thought crossed his mind, he felt a twinge of regret at the dispassionate way with which he still considered them. For all their dull predictability, they had *not* been characters in a novel; they had been real flesh and blood people who had died unnecessarily and prematurely. They ought still to have been alive; if not exactly enjoying, at least experiencing their lives. And yet, it was only a twinge of regret that he felt and it did not linger long.

Longhorne allowed himself to think more deeply about the people that he had called mother and father, tracing his memories back slowly from the evening of the fire to the earliest time he could recall being with them. He knew that they had adopted him; they had told him so, but he could not remember when they had imparted this information. Had he always been aware of it or had they broken the news to him at some point during his childhood or adolescence? He had no idea.

He could not remember how long he had lived with them; the best his memory could reveal was that he and they had been there, evening by evening in the farmhouse kitchen for at least three or four years before their deaths. He made a mental note again that he would press himself to go further back, but not now, not just yet. He wanted to come to terms, to some degree at least, with the parents that he had lost, the ones that he *could* remember.

He could easily remember their appearance, their routines and rituals… their dullness. With something of a shock he realised that he could remember virtually nothing about *them*. He knew what he could *not* say about them, but he was at a loss to know what he *could* say. He could not say if they were kind or merely dutiful. He did not know if they had truly loved him or had merely taken care of him. He could not say what their interests had been, if any; what, if anything, gave them pleasure or made them angry. He didn't know if they had such feelings or even if they were capable of having them. He realised, with something of a chill, that he didn't know them at all.

Furthermore, he continued to reason as if he were a prosecutor arguing a case before a jury, he didn't know what they felt about him or what he had felt, still felt, about them. Not quite true, he corrected himself, he knew what he felt: he felt... nothing; not warmth, not coldness, just nothing. As a matter of principle, he supposed that he 'felt' a degree of gratitude that they had given him food, shelter and the opportunity of an education. He 'felt' regret at their deaths, but even as the prosecutor's voice fell silent, he admitted in the heart of hearts that he was now discovering he possessed, he truly felt nothing: no love, no loss, no pain and no regret that his actions had led to their deaths. He knew that he ought to experience at least some of these feelings, but the new Longhorne, it seemed, was determined to be honest with himself, was unable not to be honest with himself; the truth was he felt nothing.

His next thought, once he had absorbed this brute fact, was to examine how he felt about feeling nothing. At this point, his incipient feelings began to make themselves evident. If he had felt nothing about his parents he began to feel real sorrow that he felt nothing. The sorrow swam slowly around the point in his chest where the dull ache had been; it increased in speed and intensity until it swirled around and through his chest, pushed up into his throat, stung his eyes and emerged in a sudden single cry of pain. He cried.

He cried, not for his parents, but for himself. He cried not for their loss, but for the loss of not feeling their loss. He cried because for the first time in his life that he could remember, he could.

Tears began to roll, then stream down his face, staining his shirt. He let them flow, uncaring that only a few days previously he would have been aghast at the sight he must now present. Sounds erupted from his chest, sounds that he could not recall ever hearing before and still he didn't care. He gave himself over to the tears, the feelings, the sounds. He rocked back and forth, he pounded the arms of his chair with his fists, he writhed in a catharsis of pain until he was exhausted.

Then he was still: still as an evening after a thunderstorm. He remained still, waiting to see if the storm would return. When it became apparent that it had passed he felt aware, awake, refreshed.

He moved from his armchair into the kitchen, chose one of his crystal glasses, uncorked a bottle of wine and brought them back to the living area. This, he thought to himself, was only the beginning of what might be a long night.

And so it proved to be.

It was, Longhorne thought, as he tumbled into bed around 4am the next morning, the most important night of his life. He had never been awake at 4am before; not even on the night of the fire. He knew that he would not have another night like this again in his life; there would be no need. Now he believed that he knew who and what he was; now he believed that he knew what he had to become. If the fire in the old farmhouse had heralded his purgatory, this night had witnessed his rebirth. There could now be no turning back; the new Longhorne and all the other Longhornes had given way to this, the real, the final version. He smiled and fell asleep.

Nine

When he returned to his armchair with his bottle of fine wine, Longhorne had determined to resume his search into his past. Heartened by the success of his morning enquiry and strengthened by the catharsis of his evening experience, he was ready, more than ready to face whatever he might discover of his childhood and adolescence. He felt no need to pause this fascinating journey of self-discovery. He was not to know that over the next few hours he would discover precisely nothing about his past, but more than he could possibly have ever expected to know about his future.

The session began much as he had expected: he took a few sips of wine, closed his eyes, relaxed his mind and began to drift back from the fire incident towards earlier memories. He was able to recall the sense of routine that defined his existence in the farmhouse, the routine that permeated everything. With ease, he could visualise the farmhouse, the grandfather clock in the hallway, the old-fashioned kitchen with the battered sofa at the back of the room and he could see the near-cyphers that were his parents, but he could see no further. He opened his eyes, took a few more sips of wine and tried again; again he came up against the same wall blocking the way to his childhood and early adolescence.

He could, he thought, reach back through a haze to a time when he must have been around sixteen. He wasn't sure, though, if the memory was real: maybe it was just the product of his present mind trying too hard to make something appear. That was not good enough for him; he wanted to be certain that what he was experiencing was a genuine memory and not merely a construct of his mind. A sense of being seated at the kitchen table flitted briefly through his mind and disappeared; he felt a surge of nervousness, almost of foreboding, only for it to drain rapidly away. The scent of freshly mown grass played around his nostrils only to dissipate almost as soon as it had arrived. He grasped at these sensations, but they slipped through his fingers. He felt that something had occurred, but he could get no further; there were no details, no incidents, no identifiable memories; just the background of the farmhouse and his parents' routine. He stopped trying.

He realised that there was no point in repeating the experiment. Rather than trying to get past this wall to find out what lay on the other side, he told himself that he had to try to identify what the wall was. Why was it there, why was it in the way?

He began to explore a series of thoughts. Perhaps the wall was a barrier to a childhood or adolescent trauma, as big if not bigger than the fire; perhaps it was a coping mechanism that he had employed to come to terms with the knowledge of his adoption; perhaps it was an organic thing, the result of illness or physical trauma, perhaps… perhaps it could be anything; how could he possibly know?

He took stock: what he did know for certain was that he was adopted. As soon as this thought had landed, he realised that he couldn't be certain even of that. The most he could say was that this was what his parents had told him. That assertion, too, quickly buckled under scrutiny. When he tried to pin down when and how they had told him that he had been adopted, he was at a loss. He could not recall any specific incident. He didn't know if he had always known or if the news had come as a shock; if he had been adopted at birth or at some point in his childhood. He didn't know if it had been the shock of being told that he was adopted that had caused him to block out earlier memories of childhood and adolescence or if the cause lay somewhere else entirely. He realised that he didn't really know anything about it at all: he *believed* that he had been adopted and he *believed* that his parents had told him so, but he had no memory, no evidence that either was true.

Longhorne had been prepared to accept, albeit reluctantly, that when he began his quest there was a possibility that he might not discover his true identity. He understood that his childhood might remain lost to him. He knew also that this thought had not previously troubled him, or to be more precise, it had not troubled the magnolia version of him. To be even more precise, he recognised that the thought had never entered the magnolia Longhorne's mind. *That* Longhorne had never experienced any desire to go beyond the narrow confines of his memory; indeed he had had no desire even to discover what those confines were. He had been content to live in a constricted present, with the past kept firmly locked away; that way lay peace of mind.

Now he truly wanted to press into his memories, but he found himself utterly incapable of doing so. The doors to his past seemed to have been so firmly locked that they were shut forever. It was worse than that, he reflected: he was unable even to find a door to try to push open. His past was closed away behind an impenetrable wall and it seemed that now he might also have to reconcile himself to the thought that one of the few foundations of his former life that he believed was firmly in place might have been built on quicksand.

Longhorne retraced his steps. He reviewed his first failed attempts to reach back beyond the fire incident and accepted that there was nothing new or different he could do were he to try again. He acknowledged that he could not, by sheer willpower, force his mind to open up, even though in the past, he had forced it to shut down. Adjusting to this reality, he quickly bartered that he would accept living permanently with the loss of his childhood, but he was not prepared to let go of the one thing that he believed was certain *about* his childhood. To think that it might not be true, was too challenging a thought to let slip. There had to be a way of finding out; he *had* to know. His mind raced, exploring every possible avenue. Maybe his parents had, in fact, been his parents; perhaps his mind had fashioned a false memory of his adoption as a bizarre way of creating distance between himself and his parents so that their deaths would not mean as much to him as they ought to… or perhaps he was right all along and he just wasn't able to break through the wall of his amnesia to prove it.

The wall: there it was again, measureless, unyielding, impenetrable. '*So high, you can't get over it; so low, you can't get under it, so wide you can't get round it…*'. The words and tune of what could only have been a children's song leapt out from behind the wall, giving lie to its own message. It startled Longhorne, distracting him, for the moment at least, from his quest. Where had it come from and what was it? It sounded like something halfway between a nursery rhyme and an advertising jingle, and while Longhorne was not given to listening to either, he had not been so closeted that he was unable to recognise them.

Had his mind invented this ditty? He felt a touch of shame at the thought that it might have: the words and tune were so simplistic, so predictable, so… puerile that he felt he ought to have done better. He found himself hoping that the origin of the tawdry little chant lay outside his head, but if it did, where on earth had it come from and why had it entered his mind now?

It suddenly struck him that he had a way of finding out if the nursery rhyme-cum-jingle was his or if it was a fragment of a childhood memory that had projected itself unheralded and, he felt, unwanted into his consciousness: all he had to do was consult his laptop.

The magnolia Longhorne would have acted immediately to identify and neutralise this intruder into his mind, but the new Longhorne hesitated. He had been rather enjoying his introspection, he enjoyed having to rely on his own thoughts and memories, even his own feelings; it felt like a retrograde step to resort to using technology. It was almost like cheating. Still, the tune would not leave his mind and after spending a few minutes waiting in vain to see if any further clues to its origin would emerge, he reached for his laptop, sat down at his kitchen table, logged in and typed the words into his search engine: 'So high you can't get over it'.

He had not expected to find *that*.

The words and tune did indeed belong to a children's song; more than that, they belonged to a children's 'Sunday School chorus', as the internet put it. After a few minutes of further searching, he found a video of it and his heart sank further. Longhorne had taken no interest in music or the arts, but he knew instinctively that this little song was not to his taste: not the words, not the tune, not the sentiment it expressed.

Jesus's love is very wonderful
Jesus's love is very wonderful,
Jesus's love is very wonderful,
Oh, wonderful love!
It's so high you can't get over it,
So low you can't get under it,
So wide you can't get round it,
Oh, wonderful love!

To his horror, he discovered that there were 'actions' to the words which, on the video he viewed, were enthusiastically performed by adults and children alike as they were led by a cheery, robed cleric standing at the front of an imposing classically styled church building. It seemed that one rendition of the piece was not sufficient for this particularly energetic cleric and his congregation; it was sung with increasing speed and gusto a number of times until cleric, adults and children alike had exhausted themselves, the song and Longhorne's patience. All involved appeared to be delighted with the performance; all except an organist who, perched on his organ stool at the edge of the screen and almost out of shot, spent the time shuffling through pages of music as if they and they alone could deliver him from his solitary purgatory.

Longhorne sat back from his kitchen table, pushed the laptop away and stared at it in silence. He was tempted to put himself through the ordeal once more, just in case he had missed something of note the first time, but he could not bring himself to do it. Once was enough; infinitely more than enough.

Could this really have been part of his childhood: not that particular church, he understood, but that song? If it was, how could his parents ever have agreed to him being part of such trivial inane nonsense? It was as far from anything that he associated with the memories of his parents that it underlined his conviction that he must have been adopted: his parents would never have been part of *that*. No sooner had the thought presented itself than he realised that the snatched memories of the song might have been part of a school assembly, something over which his parents could have had no control. He sighed and wondered what it meant.

Longhorne had not been religious, *was* not religious, but he was not entirely ignorant of religion. He had read about Jesus of Nazareth and about the origins, growth and development of the Christian Church, but he had read out of historical, not theological, interest, just as he had read of the origins of other religions, philosophies and political movements. His interest in the Christian Church had not been in any way notable; it was simply one topic out of many that had crossed his path without leaving much of a trace.

As a student of history, he had decided that very little could be known of the historical person known to the world as Jesus of Nazareth. What was accessible were the stories that the early Church had woven together to form the Christian Gospels, but he had not been sufficiently interested in the topic to attempt to unravel historical fact from interpretative narrative. He was aware that scholars had made entire careers out of the endeavour without having come to any consensus; he was happy to leave them to it. As for any active attachment to the religion that purported to be based on the life and teachings of Jesus: that was entirely out of the question. The magnolia Longhorne could not have allowed it to trespass into his calm, ordered world; the new Longhorne had not, up to this point, given it a thought.

All the same, he felt aggrieved by the little song and by the cheery adults who had beamed out at him from his laptop screen; adults who had decided that this should be their children's introduction to the life of Jesus.

He did not feel any affinity with the first-century prophet, but he did feel that it was disrespectful to reduce his life and memory to a trite little feel-good song. Whatever or whoever Jesus of Nazareth had been, Longhorne instinctively felt that he deserved better that that. Indeed, he reflected, Jesus of Nazareth probably deserved better than the religion that had used his name to propel itself to more than a millennium of domination in Europe and beyond and that still led sway in large swathes of the world: probably, but it wasn't a topic that had arrested his attention enough for him to have given it very much thought.

Until now. Now the wretched little song would not let go of him; it disturbed him, irritated him, offended him. The irritation and sense of offence were not entirely rational: even though in a vague way, he respected him as an historical figure, who or what was Jesus of Nazareth to him? The annoyance was also something other than a superficial feeling; it ran deep within him, it was something visceral. He recognised this even as he was at a loss to think why a vacuous piece of doggerel should have this effect. It wasn't just the words and the tune, he reflected; it wasn't even the less than innovative actions, ridiculous as they seemed to him: it was, above all, the adults singing it that he found offensive. Their grinning, jolly performance belied any truth that could possible lie behind the song; not that there was much truth likely to be found there anyway. Still, if they were in some ways followers of Jesus of Nazareth (whatever *that* meant) surely they ought to have treated him and his memory with greater respect.

Longhorne determined to close his mind to the irritation. He had not checked to see when the wretched little video had been recorded and he had no desire to subject himself to it again to find out. In any event, what was done, was done: there was nothing he could do to undo it. He could try to erase it from his mind, but he could not erase it from having happened. What they did and why they did it was of no consequence to him, he reasoned, or at least it ought to be of no consequence to him. What was of consequence was the disturbing reality that this song had come to him out of his own subconscious mind. What did that signify? What could it possibly signify?

He rationalised that somehow he must have heard the song during his childhood even though he might never be able to pinpoint when or where. He certainly had not heard it during the decade of his magnolia existence and he was fairly certain that he had not heard it during his stay in hospital, though that was a possibility that he could not entirely discount; stranger things had occurred in the background of the psychiatric hospital that had gone virtually unnoticed by his conscious mind. A fellow-patient or group of patients *could* have intoned the awful song. He dismissed the idea, although he was not quite sure why. Something told him that it had reached out to him from his own past and while he would have much preferred to have allocated it to a bed in the psychiatric hospital, he felt that he could not disown it so easily.

For it to emerge as strongly as it did, it was probably a song that he had heard more than once, perhaps numerous times. If indeed it had been a song from his childhood, he could not tell whether at that time he had found the song attractive or irritating or just a song that was there. He didn't know if he sang it himself or, if he had, whether he sang it with pleasure or distaste. What a banal, stupid, irritating thing for his memory to disgorge.

Still it would not let him go. Why had his memory regurgitated only part of the song? Was it because that part was applicable to the imagery of the wall that he had viewed as obstructing access to his memories of childhood or was it because he harboured an antipathy, perhaps even a revulsion, to the song's religious theme? Again, it seemed to him, there was no way of finding out. Perhaps he was simply thinking too deeply about it; perhaps it was no more than a silly little song without any real significance for him. With a sinking heart, he knew that was not the case.

He decided to test the strength of the wall one more time. After all, if the song had somehow made its way past the wall's defences, perhaps something else could be liberated as well. Maybe the song was the key to breaking through the wall; perhaps it could open up a small hole in its defences, allowing more memories to trickle through. Perhaps the trickle would become a stream and then a torrent; it was worth another try.

Longhorne settled himself back in his armchair. After a moment's hesitation, he took a few more sips of wine; he reassured himself that his mind was clear and unaffected; he simply wanted to feel a little more relaxed.

He began to think about the song, but his irritation at it quickly resurfaced. He tried a different tactic. Much as he disliked it, he allowed the tune and the words to play over and over again in his head without paying attention to their meaning. He could not bring himself to picture the grinning adults or the slightly manic cleric, but the song itself he could just about face. Still nothing emerged.

A new thought struck him. If the song was a genuine memory and he had either sung it or had heard it sung, then perhaps he needed to sing it to jog other memories. He recoiled at the thought; he objected, he rebelled. That, he scolded himself, was much more than a step too far. He persisted with his original approach; still nothing peeked from behind the wall.

With a groan, he succumbed to the inevitable: he began to sing along in his mind to the song. The words were seared on his consciousness, not that they were difficult to remember. The tune threatened to shred his nerves with its skippy, jumpy rhythm and its simple, predictable, undulating melody. Over and over again he silently sang along to the tune; to his annoyance the result was the same.

With a chill, he realised that he had not exhausted all options available to him: there was yet one further step that he could take: he could sing aloud. He protested; he felt like standing up and walking out of the room in protest. He could not remember ever singing aloud, never mind singing a song like *that*. He would not do it; he would not participate in the idiocy of the lyrics; he would not be complicit in the inanity, in the disrespect of the song. He *could* not do it.

The words began to tumble from his lips, almost in spite of himself.

It happened again.

Ten

This time it was different. Longhorne didn't see anything, he didn't hear anything; instead he found himself inside a mind that wasn't his own. He was aware simultaneously of thinking thoughts that were not his while also somehow being an observer of them. He was able to note the passage of the thoughts as they coursed through his mind, but he was so intimately connected to them that they felt as if they were his own; yet he knew that they weren't. Afterwards, he tried to think of an analogy to describe the experience to himself, but he couldn't find an appropriate one. The nearest he could manage was to liken it to listening to a voice on the radio that sounded very much like his own, but wasn't, and being so absorbed by what was being said that he had no capacity for reaction or analysis. He was aware that the thoughts running through his mind were not his, but he could neither stop them from flowing nor could he comment on them to himself. They were not his thoughts, yet he was one with them.

It was not only the other mind's thoughts that he

was one with; he was also one with its feelings, emotions and with something else indefinable: a sense of *being* that was not his, but which so imposed itself upon him that he felt it impossible to think of himself as separate or apart from this other being, this other mind. Unlike his experience in the library, which was still masked from his mind, he felt neither startled nor afraid; this seemed the most natural thing in the world to experience, the most natural thing in the world to *be*. All desire to explore his childhood and adolescence had fallen away from him. His past, his identity did not matter; all that mattered now was the oneness he felt with the other mind.

It *was* another mind, but the otherness consisted entirely of him being able to observe his union with it. There was nothing alien about it, nothing that caused him to want to retreat from it. If it were possible, he wanted to be absorbed not only by what it was thinking; but he wanted to be absorbed by *it*. He had a deep sense of being totally, fully at home.

The thoughts and the feelings that filled his mind were not uniformly comforting, but the experience of being one with them was. Longhorne had never considered himself to have any mystical abilities or pretensions, but as he thought later of how the other mind had enveloped him, encapsulated him, *incorporated* him, he acknowledged that his experience could be classified by others to lie somewhere within the realms of mysticism. That was not how it felt to him, however. Mysticism, as he understood it, necessitated embracing some form of mental, even spiritual, discipline in order to attain an altered state of consciousness. As far as he could tell, he had done nothing to prepare his mind for this experience; it simply happened. It was not something that he had achieved; it was something given to him.

While Longhorne's experience was a unified whole, it also consisted of discreet moments, each blending into the others seamlessly, organically. Thus it was, that the smallest fraction of a second before he became aware of any thoughts entering his consciousness, he became aware of the sense of oneness with the other mind (which, predictable as it was, he later found himself terming 'the Other') and with that sense came a sea of feelings that remained constant throughout the experience.

Longhorne had been a stranger to feelings for so much of his life, having begun to rediscover them only a few days previously, that he struggled at first to recognise what they all were. It took him a few moments to monitor, identify and log these emotions, but he was certain that they were all there all of the time. Unlike his normal experience, these feelings did not change, develop or fade; one did not follow the other. They were timeless, fully present and consistent. They did not compete with one another or call out for attention; they were simply there, as real, as fundamental as the laws of physics. They formed the backdrop to his existence; more than that, he felt, they were the tectonic plates that undergirded all existence, shifting and moving, perhaps, but always there.

The feelings varied in intensity from one another: some deep and foundational, some light and close to the surface, though each individual feeling remained constant within itself. It seemed as if they had a pulse that gave them life and vitality, yet he was not aware of any ebb or flow in their potency as they swept through his mind. He could identify each feeling, yet it was not quite right to speak of the feelings as being individual, as if one could exist, could *ever* have existed, without the others; they combined, coalesced together to form a whole, all-encompassing experience of existence; they defined what it was to be living, to be conscious, to *be*.

He was constantly aware of a deep, fathomless sorrow, of lightning stabs of fear, of limitless expansions of peace, of boundless love and of bubbling effervescent joy. Pain beyond comprehension mixed fully, readily with pleasure beyond description; despair intertwined intimately with hope. Had he been able to employ his rational mind he would have told himself that it was impossible to experience all of these feelings simultaneously, but his rational mind had been supplanted; he *knew* the reality of these feelings, he sensed their completeness and he understood that in their own singularity and even more so in combination with one another, they formed the very essence of reality, a reality that undergirded and surpassed thought, sensory experience and the passage of time.

For an instant he was eternal.

For more than an instant, perhaps: throughout the experience, which he subsequently realised lasted for more than five hours he retained this sense of being eternal. When he thought about it later, however, he recognised that, during the 'event' he was oblivious to the passage of time; there was no 'during' to speak of. At the very deepest level, this sense of being that had overwhelmed him and all other elements of the experience *were* encapsulated in an instant; it was as if he inhabited an eternal present when all things that had been and would ever be simply... were.

A flicker of a moment after he became aware of the feelings and the sense of oneness with the other mind he became aware of the thoughts. Again, he reflected afterwards, it was probably wrong to say that the thoughts came after the feelings in a temporal sense at all; that was merely his mind's way of trying to interpret the uninterpretable. The feelings and especially the sense of oneness with the Other came first, not temporally, but existentially.

Unlike the feelings and *the feeling of being*, the thoughts *were* sequential or to be more precise he remembered them as if they had been sequential. Perhaps they too had simply 'been' there. Afterwards, he wondered if the impression of sequence was the result of his own mind being incapable of thinking in any other way. Perhaps the Other's mind thought eternally, just as it felt eternally; perhaps he was so tied to his own processes of thought that he was unable to enter the thoughts of the Other as fully as he had entered into the Other's feeling. Perhaps his inexperience of embracing his own feelings, his own emotions had enabled him to be open to the Other in that area in a way that his well-trained rational mind did not allow when it came to following the Other's thoughts. He did not know and it did not trouble him; it was a matter of little consequence compared to the richness, the fullness of the experience.

The thoughts came to him as a stream of consciousness. They were not neatly ordered or edited. It was as if a floodgate in the Other's mind had been opened wide and everything, *everything*, that the Other was thinking poured out. The thoughts, like the feelings, were varied to the point of apparent contradiction. They were direct, subtle, complex, simple, sly, honest, cowardly and fearless, combining to form a captivating kaleidoscope of consciousness. The mind of the Other stood above them, faced them boldly, embraced them, making no attempt to hide or suppress them. The mind of the Other was a mind that was as completely and absolutely free as it was courageous; it was unchained, unleashed, exuberant in its liberty and ruthless in its candour.

Longhorne felt that in its openness and in its sense of adventure, the mind of the Other could not have been more different from his own mind, from the mind of any of the sequences of Longhornes that he had known, that he had *been*. Paradoxically, the Other's mind also felt utterly familiar to him, more familiar than he had ever felt his own mind to be. The mind of the Other was his mind as it *ought to be*, as he wanted it to be, as he needed it to be.

It seemed to Longhorne that as it took him a moment to tune into the thoughts of the Other it was rather like tuning into the old-fashioned radio that had stood on the kitchen mantelpiece in his parents' farmhouse. This was partly because, as with his own mind, the Other's mind was thinking at a number of levels simultaneously. At a basic level, the Other seemed to be responding semi-automatically to things that the Other could see and feel that were hidden from Longhorne. He was in the Other's mind, but while it seemed that the Other had a body, Longhorne did not feel that he was within *it* or if he was, he was not privy to its senses. At a more conscious level, the Other was articulating thoughts. To be more accurate, Longhorne experienced the thoughts as articulations; articulations in a foreign, at times guttural language which somehow he understood perfectly. He was aware that he had heard this language before, that he had understood it then too. Silently, easily, for the first time since it had occurred, the memory of the library incident came back to him; this time there was no fear, no panic. In the library, it was as if he had looked through the Other's eyes and heard through the Other's ears; now he was *in* the Other's mind. He now realised also that his ecstatic dream, the thing that had set off this whole process of illumination and discovery, had also been an introduction to the Other. He knew all this in a flash of insight; how foolish he had been to rationalise it; how pale and empty his theories now appeared. He did not castigate himself, however, for his previous dullness of mind; he simply accepted that he had been wrong and moved onward, captivated by the Other's mind.

Somewhere above and beyond the articulated thoughts, the Other retained a calm control: monitoring, analysing, deciding. The Other was calm and self-aware, yet did not seem aloof or detached from his 'lower' levels of thought or from the swirl of feelings that formed the continuous backdrop to all that was. Longhorne was aware of this, following every thought, every reflection; he was aware also that his own mind lay superimposed on all of this, but that it was unable by itself to do anything other than experience and then observe its own experience.

The Other was in pain: not physical pain, but intense mental and emotional pain. A thousand thoughts flashed before Longhorne's mind, some half-formed, some beginning and then ending abruptly, some doggedly persisting until the control part of the Other's mind selected them for consideration or dismissed them with a resolute finality. Each of the thoughts carried with them their own feelings and emotions, different from the deep-seated mixture of emotions than remained constant, but these, Longhorne sensed, had themselves played a role in creating that experience of eternal existence.

Angry thoughts questioned 'why?', sad thoughts proclaimed that the end of the Other's existence was approaching, defiant thoughts raised their heads and called on enemies to do their worst. A rising tide of fear was ruthlessly suppressed by an act of willpower that pushed it down beyond a place where Longhorne could either find or follow it. Slowly, the cascade of thoughts lessened; the Other took control and for a time order was restored.

Memories swam to the surface; memories of friends' laughter, memories of enemies' insults and accusations; memories, too, of home and childhood: warm, safe, cossetted. Of these memories Longhorne sensed only the Other's thoughts and feelings. He did not share in any visualisation of them that the Other might have had; he did not know why. There were no faces, no colours, no sounds: just thoughts and feelings. He sensed that some sort of barrier was stopping him from entering more fully into the mind of the Other, although no such barrier was blocking him from absorbing the deep sense of oneness, of integration, that lay at the vortex of the Other's feelings. Again, he did not know why there seemed to be a disparity between his complete ability to experience the Other's feelings and his partial ability to follow the Other's thoughts. The barrier, he felt, was not an impenetrable wall: one small push, perhaps, and it would collapse. Not yet, however, not yet; he understood that the time was not quite right.

As the Other reflected on a childhood memory that brought with it a heart-tugging sense of closeness and love, a sudden dark and violent trust of panic lunged into focus. It overwhelmed the Other's defences, threatened to capture the Other's soul, to usurp the Other's mind. The Other screamed at it, first out of terror and then from pain. The panic consumed the Other, fear, doubt, self-loathing were everywhere. An abyss opened up in the Other's mind; empty, bottomless, eternal. The Other recoiled, yet felt bound, unable to move, helpless before it. Swirling, reeling, the Other began to fall.

The fall was stopped; not by the Other's mind or willpower, but by something deep within the Other, deeper still than the source of fear, pain and panic. It swept the Other up, carried the Other to a place of rescue, respite and safety, a place of calm and clear reflection, a place of healing. Longhorne felt as if he were about to be blown apart by this magnificent, glorious intervention and by whatever it was that intervened. A wave of what he could only describe as bliss swept over him as it swept over the Other. He had never known such ecstasy, not even during his dream.

The Other had reached a point of truth, of oneness, of integration with something that was both beyond and within the essence of being (unable to think of a better term, Longhorne later resorted to terming it 'the Unity'). The oneness, reached to all things within and beyond the Universe, to things sentient, to things that previously had seemed to Longhorne to be unimportant, redundant, inert. The harmonies of all things resounded within the Unity and swept from the Unity to the Other and then from the Other to Longhorne. They existed in a song, a dance, a drama that was both constantly changing and unfurling and yet was quite complete. For the briefest of moments, Longhorne knew himself to be one harmony within the song, one movement within the dance, one actor in the drama. At the same time, he understood that he was more than just a single harmony, more even than one harmony joined and blended with others: he was the entire score, the entire dance, the entire drama. It might have lasted less than a second, but for that brief time, Longhorne and the Other and the Unity and all things that ever were and ever could be were completely, inseparably one. The bliss was momentary, but its effect lingered as it gave way to a clarity of mind and purpose that Longhorne did not know, could never have guessed, was attainable.

The Other, too, felt and knew the clarity. The Other's thoughts had now passed beyond the point of being calm and ordered; they were resolute, certain, filled with conviction. The Other no longer monitored, analysed and acted as an arbiter of thought; the knowledge of all things and the decision that flowed from being one with all things were as inexorable as the turning of the planets, as the warmth of the sun. Longhorne felt the Other's thought, the Other's determination, the Other's resolve. They resounded and echoed within him.

With a knowledge deeper than any he had ever experienced, Longhorne knew that he was in the mind of Christ.

Eleven

At the time, Longhorne had no idea how long he spent absorbing the realisation that the Other's mind was that of Jesus; more than that, it was the mind of Jesus at a particular point in his life. He knew enough about the reputed life of Jesus to recognise that he had witnessed his Gethsemane experience. As the realisation hit him, time seemed to stop: no further thoughts flowed, no further words emerged. He sat still, his mind full of one thought only: he had experienced the moment of Jesus's commitment to fulfil his mission, not as an outside observer might, but from within, from within Jesus himself. The thought absorbed him fully. Had it been possible, he later reflected, he would have happily stayed in that state for a lifetime; it was, for him, a moment of heart-stopping revelation.

The moment, however, did not last a lifetime. When Longhorne felt the feeling of union beginning to lift from him, he opened his eyes and they fell on the old-style clock hanging on his lounge wall. It told him that it was almost four o'clock in the morning.

Without hesitation, he knew that it was time to sleep, not because he felt tired, but because he felt satisfied, satiated with life. He no longer felt any struggle within or any need to explore his life any further. He did not need to know how or why he had become the persons he had been; what mattered now was the person he was and the person he was becoming. His past was of no significance to him; his future was everything. He was no longer the magnolia Longhorne or even the new Longhorne; he was Longhorne reborn.

When he woke later that morning at what was for him the hitherto unthinkably late hour of 10am, he felt no urgency to move from his bed to go about the business of his day. He allowed his head to remain resting on his pillow and welcomed the thoughts that flowed through it.

He remembered every detail of the experience of the night before. So much of the past few weeks began to fall into place in his mind. The dream and the experience in the library, he realised, were flashbacks to events in the life of Jesus as he, himself, had experienced them.

He had no idea how or why he had accessed the mind of Jesus or if he could just as readily have found himself accessing the mind of another person either living or dead. He had no knowledge of the mechanism by which the experience had come to him; he simply knew that it had and he felt privileged that such had been the case. He also had no idea if he was alone in having such an experience; perhaps the world was full of fellow mind-travellers. He reflected that he was unlikely to find out if this were so, but the thought did not linger: he was much too interested in his own journey to think any more about it.

He had been inside the mind of Jesus, but he still preferred to call him 'the Other' in recognition that it was more than an historical person that he had touched. Within the greater reality of the Unity, the Other was a complete, timeless person. He sensed that, in conjunction with them, *in union*, with them, so too was he.

He mused that the feeling in his chest that had at first perturbed him and then had become something that he had welcomed was testament to the truth of a deep reality within: he was not an isolated human being; he was intrinsically, fundamentally united to the Other and through this union he was joined to what lay beyond the Other, to the greater reality that had infused the Other's mind: to the Unity.

He remembered too, the sense of wholeness that had encapsulated the Other's deep emotional life, the sense of connectedness that integrated all feeling and all experience. He felt that in some way this connected him not only to the Other and to the Unity, but it connected him to all things, to all people... to everything.

As he lay on his bed, these thoughts swept through his mind, but he was aware that they were *his* thoughts. Not that he understood where his thoughts came from any more than he understood the source of the Other's thoughts, he reasoned: they simply appeared from somewhere in his mind and introduced themselves to him. As with the mind of the Other, he could observe and monitor them, he could arbitrate and choose which thoughts to follow or dismiss, but he could not make his thoughts happen and he could not stop them from occurring. They were intrinsic to him and yet they also seemed to have something of a life of their own. Perhaps both his thoughts and the thoughts of the Other, of Christ, had the same source; perhaps they were only in part their thoughts, emanations of a greater mind that they could colour and flavour, but not determine fully. Maybe that was why he could enter the mind of Christ; they were both part of a greater mind, perhaps that of the Unity... or maybe not. Longhorne could not tell what the truth might be or even how he might find out what it was, but he enjoyed toying with the ideas; toying with his own mind now that it was open to him.

He tried a little thought experiment. He told his mind to recite the dates of the births and deaths of all the kings and queens of England between the Norman Conquest and the Civil War. His mind churned out the information as he knew it would. He could command his brain to perform a task that he knew it should be competent to perform, but he knew that this particular choice of task was something that had just popped into his mind, just as had the decision to perform the thought experiment in the first place. He believed that he could have decided not to perform the thought experiment or that he could have rejected the particular experiment that his brain had selected and asked it to come up with another, but that selection or its alternatives were not things over which he could exercise any choice. He tried again.

He asked his brain to inform him of the names of the other people living in his apartment building. It drew a blank as he knew it would; it could not provide information that he had not lodged there. The decision not to learn the names of his neighbours was his; or was it? He had felt compelled to live an isolated, insular life as a reaction to his earlier experiences. Had he truly made a voluntary decision to live as a virtual hermit? What real degree of control did he have over his actions, never mind his thoughts?

He smiled at the mental games that he was playing with himself. He knew that he was asking important questions, ones that philosophers, psychologists and neuroscientists had puzzled over for decades, but he had no interest in pursuing them, at least not at that point. He was content to acknowledge idly that no matter how deeply he might think that he knew himself and the workings of his mind, he didn't really know very much at all. How then could he expect to know much about the mind of the Other, the mind of Christ, unless it was revealed to him?

He went back to focusing his mind on the previous night's event. He tried to recall it, recognising again that the experience was at one and the same time a single unified 'happening' and also a multi-faceted series of thoughts, impressions and sensations. Not so much a series, he decided, as one layer of existence placed on top of another, but in such a way that all layers were both instantly visible and yet discreet, like a three-dimensional chess set.

He was also acutely aware that his reflections were precisely that: reflections on what had happened; they were not a re-enactment of it. They came close to the experience, but they were neither the experience itself nor a re-run of it. He recognised that the experience, too, was something that he had no control over; it had a dynamic of its own. It began and concluded as it (or some other hand) had determined. The same had been true of the dream and the library 'vision'. He could not make them happen and he could not make them stop once they had begun. He did not know if he would have another similar experience again and if he did what it might reveal or when it might come, but he knew that he could do nothing either to make it happen or to avoid it happening if it came his way. He was quite content with the thought.

After a while, he got up, showered and prepared what was either a late breakfast or an early lunch; he could not decide which. He glanced at the walls of his apartment and decided that he would complete the painting of his living room and kitchen; it seemed to him to be the most natural thing in the world to do for someone who had just been inside the mind of Jesus of Nazareth.

It did not cross his mind to doubt his identification of the Other. He knew enough of the Gospel stories to recognise the outline of Jesus's life: the accounts of his baptism, his controversies with religious and political authorities, and the events that led to his death were lightly etched into his memory even if he was uncertain whether they were truly historical events or not. His identification of the Other as Jesus, however, did not come from that background knowledge; it was something given to him, something that he just knew. At no point did he pause to doubt either his sanity or the reality of his experience.

Similarly, he did not doubt that his experience was one in which he had genuinely been inside the mind of Jesus; it was neither a dream nor a product of his imagination. The mind he had found himself occupying really was the mind of Jesus. Or perhaps it was the other way round, he pondered for a moment: maybe the mind of Jesus, as a manifestation of the timeless Other, had somehow occupied his mind, though it would be even harder to understand how such could be the case. Either way, he understood that he had absolutely no explanation for his experience: it simply had happened. There it was: take it or leave it, and Longhorne found himself taking it wholeheartedly. He marvelled a little at how natural, how matter-of-fact this identification had been and how easy it was for him to absorb this new reality in the warm light of day, but the experience itself was beyond doubt and beyond questioning; it was now an integral part of him.

As he moved the paint roller backwards and forwards, he dismissed such ruminations from his mind. He was glad to take delight in watching the paint bubble, burst, glisten and then blend into the walls of his home. He enjoyed the smell, he enjoyed the way he could feel the undulations and imperfections of the plaster under the roller, and he enjoyed the sense of achievement when the job was completed. Who could have known that such a simple act could be so fulfilling?

He had finished his painting halfway through the afternoon. Longhorne decided that he needed some fresh air. It was too late in the day to go to his park, though he decided that he would spend some time in it tomorrow. Today, he chose to do something that he had never done before: he would take a walk around his neighbourhood. He would open his eyes and his mind to it; he would explore it.

It was a bright, warm afternoon so he had no need of either a coat or umbrella. He felt a little over-dressed in his suit, but having discarded his customary tie he felt that his dress now mirrored a little more closely his new-found sense of freedom. He made a mental note that he ought to consider buying some new clothes; clothes that, like the colours of his freshly painted lounge, would better reflect who and what he now felt himself to be. That, he knew, would be a daunting prospect, one that would take him into entirely new territory, demanding a series of conversations and interactions that he was not quite sure that he was ready for. Nonetheless, he refused to discount the thought; he would return to it later.

He closed the door of his apartment building behind him without a backward glance and looked at his surroundings. He saw the familiar path to the bus stop, saw the street lights without feeling any compulsion to count them and he saw people moving about, intent on their business. That in itself was unusual. He had, of course, known that other people lived in his neighbourhood and that, like him, they walked or drove to and from their homes, their work-places, their shops and places of leisure, but he had never taken note of them before. They had been less than the lamp-posts to him; too erratic and unpredictable to count, not quite worth noticing. Now he saw them with something he realised approached genuine interest.

Longhorne's interest went beyond noting the superficial outlines of his neighbours' bodies and clothing. He observed the way they walked or stood as they waited for a bus, how most of them looked down at the ground or at their phones rather than at their surroundings or at others. He saw how disconnected they were from one another and from their environment; he knew that just a few short days ago he would have acted no differently from them except instead of looking at a phone he would have been routinely counting lamp-posts, paving stones and trees.

He noted also how few of them were in conversation, either directly or on their phones, with someone else. One or two appeared to be texting, but mostly they were flicking idly through their screens or staring listlessly into the middle-distance. Away from the bus stop, on a piece of green close to where the smart apartments gave way to even smarter houses a group of children played, their voices rising and settling in the breeze. They, at least, showed signs of engagement, signs of life.

Longhorne was surprised at the feeling of mild irritation that began to tug at him as he scanned his neighbours. Such a feeling was unreasonable, he knew, given that until that moment he had shown no interest in them, their lives or their homes; why should they have been any different from the magnolia Longhorne? Why should he feel irritated by them and their lack of engagement?

One reason, he thought, was that, in spite of appearances, it seemed his magnolia life had not really been so very different from the lives of those around him after all. He was not the only magnolia one; he was surrounded by people living magnolia lives. Without thinking about it very much, Longhorne had assumed that he was distinctively different from other people. He had not minded being different, it had not caused him any distress and he had had no desire to change any part of his life in order to 'fit in' with others. Now he realised that he was not really very different at all; he felt strangely cheated, robbed of his oddness. Without ever acknowledging it to himself, even as he had followed a rigid path of non-introspection, he had taken a mild, perverse satisfaction in his isolation; he had, he now noted, rather hoped that others would have been aware of his solitary station. He felt a little peeved that, clearly, they hadn't been. To them he had been nothing more than a cypher: less than a number to be counted.

Longhorne's irritation went deeper, however, than the mild annoyance he felt at his realisation that he had probably gone unnoticed by his neighbours. He understood that he had awakened from a long slumber to discover that life had colour and light; he had emerged from a self-imposed coma that was the result of the trauma of the farmhouse fire and its aftermath. There had been a reason for his social isolation, a rationale behind his protective self-absorption; what reason, what excuse, could *they* possibly have for living as if life were colourless and drab? He doubted that they could all have undergone the type of trauma that he had endured. What reason did they have for shutting down emotionally, separating themselves from one another, from life? The feelings of irritation intensified, warming to something approaching anger. Unaccustomed to such emotions, he pushed them away uncomfortably.

Perhaps he was being too hard on them, he reflected; perhaps he was reading too much into his initial observances. After all, how much could one really tell from looking at people standing at a bus stop or walking to and from their homes? Still, he shook his head at the thought; he knew that he was right: there was a fundamental problem, a deep-rooted, foundational flaw in the people he saw. No doubt, they were capable of springing into life from time to time: at a football match or in a bar or even intermittently in their own homes, but their default mode was one of disconnected listlessness.

He sensed this rather than saw it. He was not adept at reading body language; he did not even know if he was adept at understanding many of the myriad nuances of spoken language, but something that came from within each person and that permeated their entire beings called out to him, unsettled him, caused him on the one hand to want to examine them more closely while on the other, to turn from them in despair. No, despair was not the right word, that implied a level of identification that he did not feel; if he were to be honest with himself he wanted to turn from them in distaste.

All except the children; they had not yet sought cover under the opaque canopy that sheltered and shaded everyone else, they had not yet decided to shield their eyes from the light.

Longhorne was not comfortable admitting his true feelings towards the people he had been observing. His mood changed from irritation and rising anger to sadness: sadness, in part for his neighbours, but sadness also for himself. Without admitting it to himself, he had wanted to find some common ground with people, he had hoped to discover ways of building bridges into their lives after his decade of self-imposed exile. Now it looked as if he was going to be disappointed. He walked past the bus stop again, looking at the faces; no faces looked back. He made his way along the pathway between the neatly tended bushes and shrubs that led to the green area where the children were playing. He watched them as they ran in heedless circles, chasing one another, being caught only to circle once again in games of escape and pursuit. They did not notice him, not because they were incapable of noticing him, but because they were intent on noticing one another. They, at least, were alive; perhaps he could build some bridges to them.

Longhorne walked morosely along the paths of his neighbourhood for an hour. Everywhere the reaction was the same. He would look at the faces of the adults, of the adolescents and they would register... nothing. It was not as if they found his stares strange or unsettling; he would have understood perfectly if that had been the case. They simply did not notice him at all; he might as well have been invisible.

Slowly he noticed a change in his attitude. The feelings of distaste began to fade and were replaced with feelings of loneliness, of isolation. The magnolia Longhorne had actively sought isolation, but he had never encountered loneliness; now the reborn Longhorne became aware of its bitter taste.

He had not known that he could be moved by others in this way; that their emptiness could reach into his own soul and touch it with their ice. No, not ice: that would have been definite; attractive or repellent. They were neither hot nor cold: they were tepid. He found that more repellent, more chilling than any ice bath. Even though the day was still warm, he began to wish that he had worn a coat. That would have been pointless, he reasoned: it would not have kept him from the cold that he now felt.

He returned to his apartment, wanting to feel its welcome and its warmth. The colour of his living room cheered him. He made a mental note that he would apply the bright yellow paint to the hall as soon as he could. He had never thought that his apartment could be a source of comfort, let alone cheerfulness to him. It had always been something of a refuge, a hiding place from the world, albeit a rather soulless one; now it took on a new and important dimension: it was a place of refreshment, a place for him to be revitalised. It was *home*.

Longhorne knew that all of these thoughts ought to have been foreign to him. Only a few days before, he had been unaware of everything that he had noticed during his neighbourhood walk. At the same time he also knew that they were entirely natural for him as he now was. What he was now, seemed to him to be what he always should have been, perhaps even what he really always had been deep down, but had been unaware of. Alluring as it was, he cut short this metaphysical introspection before he fell under its charm. For the time being he was content to contrast his new awakened nature with his old slumbering one and he was content to reflect that he could no more change his new nature than he had been able, on his own, to change his old.

He was quite satisfied with that thought. He acknowledged for a moment that he might change again. He had not controlled the things that had caused the changes within him to occur; it stood to reason that he would not be able to control future events either. It was possible that they, too, would change him; perhaps back to the magnolia Longhorne, perhaps to something worse, perhaps to something even better.

He accepted that the possibility existed, but discarded it as being entirely hypothetical. There was no point in expending mental or emotional energy on it. If it happened, it happened. Not that he really thought it would: he had a settled feeling that the change within him was something so fundamental, so visceral that it was unchangeable. He might not have fathomed who or what he was, but he believed that whoever or whatever he was, he had now connected with it and recognised it as his true self. There would be, there could be, no turning back for him.

He sank into the armchair and looked steadily out through the window of his living room. A small, fluffy cloud drifted past, outlined against the blue sky. He was, he thought for the first time in his life, a very lucky man.

Twelve

The next morning, Longhorne went to the park. He had prepared coffee and sandwiches, though he did not bring as much with him as usual as he had decided to break his customary habit of staying in the park all day; he would leave before lunch-time to go into town and buy some new clothes.

The park was unusually busy with more children present than he had expected; perhaps it was a school holiday, he reflected, without giving it too much thought. He had never taken any notice of such things and he thought it unlikely that would change even for the new Longhorne; attaining knowledge of the school calendar was not high on his list of priorities. The children in the park were intent on exploring pathways through the undergrowth or walking alongside their parents. They were as unaware of him as he would have been of them a few days before.

Instead of pacing around the lake as usual, he had chosen to occupy a park bench under the trees where a week or so before he had noted the anglers going about their business. It was a warm, sunny morning and the trees offered him shade without creating any chill. He was content to sit and watch the lake, not thinking about anything in particular, but not lapsing into the stupor of mindlessness that had been his previous practice unless something had been troubling his mind. He was, he realised, in a very contented frame of mind.

He chose to observe: to watch small birds as they busied to and from the branches of the trees above his head, to note other larger birds as they glided along the lake's surface. He had no idea what they were; ornithology had never been listed among his interests, but they interested him now. He was relieved and pleased to note that this interest did not transform itself into a feeling of compulsion to research them once he returned to his apartment; he simply enjoyed watching them: watching them as unique embodiments of the same life, the same spirit, that was embodied in himself.

He wasn't sure how long he sat in this preoccupied state, but after some time he became aware of a noise coming from amongst the grass and bushes behind him. At first he ignored it, thinking that it was some woodland animal. The noise persisted, however, until he felt the need to turn to see if he could identify its source.

When he did, he saw a small girl in a summer dress and wide-brimmed hat moving among the trees. She was gathering wildflowers, looking inordinately pleased with herself with each new acquisition. While no expert, Longhorne guessed that she might have been four or five years old. Looking a little more closely, Longhorne concluded that, as far as he could tell, she was probably a child with Down's syndrome; this thought registering in his mind without any definable impact.

Longhorne knew little about this condition, but he had been sufficiently engaged with the world around him to know of its existence. He had a vague understanding of its chromosomal cause, but beyond that, he knew virtually nothing.

The little girl sensed that she was being watched and turned to look at Longhorne. She smiled and walked over to him. Silently, she sat down beside him on the bench and offered him her bunch of flowers.

Longhorne had no idea how to react. Hesitantly, he smiled back, reached out his hand and took the flowers from her. Immediately her expression changed; her face flushed and her bottom lip began to tremble. Instinctively, Longhorne handed the flowers back and the girl giggled with delight. She repeated the process a few times, with the threatened tears clearly part of a delicious game that she had devised. Having exhausted its potential, she then sat quietly beside him for a moment before giving him a hug and resting her head against his side.

Longhorne could not remember when anyone had last given him a hug; he could not be sure that anyone ever had. He did not return the gesture; he wasn't quite sure how he should go about it, but inside he felt a warmth that he had not experienced before. He touched the little girl's arm lightly, then let it rest there.

Together they sat in silence, looking at the lake, looking at the birds and occasionally looking at each other. Each time their eyes met, they smiled at one another and then went back to their quiet vigil.

They sat in comfortable silence for five to ten minutes before Longhorne heard the voices. They were coming from along the path, around a bend that followed an indent in the lake shore. They sounded flustered, insistent, concerned. They were calling a name with increasing urgency. With a start, Longhorne realised that they were calling for his young companion, that they probably belonged to her parents and that she must have wandered from them. The child looked unconcerned, oblivious of their calls; she sat pressed to his side, staring dreamily across the lake with a quiet smile playing on her lips. Longhorne smiled too; they would be pleased to see that she was not lost, but sitting with him.

A couple burst around the corner, their faces etched with worry. Longhorne saw their faces, saw their expression change from worry to relief and then from relief to uncertainty. Without speaking a word the child's mother (or so Longhorne assumed her to be) hoisted the child into her arms and hugged her close to her chest. No rebuke was given to the child, but as she turned from Longhorne her expression was one of distrust.

Longhorne looked at the child's father; a man around his own age and build. He was about to comment that the child had been sitting safely with him for some time, but the man's cold stare halted the words in his throat. How odd, Longhorne thought, that instead of expressing relief he seemed to be struggling with anger. The two men looked at each other for longer than Longhorne had ever looked at anyone. The man made to speak, then stopped, then tried again and stopped again. Finally he pointed his finger slowly at Longhorne's face before lowering it just as slowly. He turned abruptly and walked away, following his wife and child back along the path.

Longhorne was perplexed. He had understood well enough that the child's parents had been worried that she was lost or perhaps, even worse, had fallen into the lake. They were not to know, he reasoned, that the lake shore was uniformly shallow and posed no danger to anyone who stumbled into its waters. When they saw the little girl sitting safely and comfortably with him, he had expected them to express relief, maybe even gratitude that he was with her. He did not expect the reaction he had just witnessed.

Not for an instant did he think that they might have perceived him as a threat to their child's safety or even as the cause of her temporary disappearance. It wasn't that he was unaware of the reality of child abduction; it was simply that he knew that he would never, *could* never, do such a thing. Surely no one could imagine that he would be capable of it either; he clearly wasn't that sort of person. It took him some time to realise that that was precisely what the child's parents had been thinking, but in the absence of evidence to back up their suspicions they had failed to say anything.

When the thought finally did strike him, he was appalled: appalled that anyone could think that of him. He knew, of course, that to the child's parents he was just a stranger; they could not know anything of his character or his motives, but the thought still stung. He felt like running after them to protest his innocence, but thought better of it. What would he have said that might not have made matters worse? The memory of the aftermath of the fire came back to him with a rush of panic. He had done nothing wrong then and he had certainly done nothing wrong now. Drawing on his previous experience, he determined to do nothing that might attract further attention to himself.

Strangely, the panic soon subsided to be replaced by a feeling of sadness. He was sad that the child's parents could not see what the child had sensed and had seen: her own innocence reflected in him. Slowly, the sadness also lifted and a mellow feeling of contentment suffused him once more. He knew that the child had touched his soul instinctively, knowing that there was nothing to fear from him. More than that, she had recognised that with him she was safe; she was at home. What did it matter if her parents had been suspicious of him; her soul was deeper than theirs; it had not yet been corrupted.

He realised that he felt the same way about her. Something about the way she had rested against him told him that more than their bodies had touched; their souls had also made contact. He was not surprised by this; after all, both his soul and hers were part of a greater whole: part of a Universal something that he had come to recognise. The memory of his sublime experience was fresh and coloured his every thought. Both he and the little girl were one with the Other and one with the Unity that encompassed all. In spite of her parents' reaction he was glad that they had met, glad that they had touched; glad that she had found him.

He looked down at the bench where the child had been sitting and noticed that she had dropped the bunch of flowers she had spent so much time gathering. Had the circumstances been different, he would had sought her out to return them, but he had enough presence of mind to know that his actions might have been misinterpreted by her parents. Instead he picked them up, placed them under his jacket next to his heart and with a noticeably light step made his way to the park exit and from there, to the bus that brought him back to his apartment.

Once there, he placed the flowers in a container of water. He did not own a vase, but he pressed one of his wine decanters into service, placing it on his windowsill. He decided that when he returned from his shopping expedition later that afternoon, he would enjoy viewing them sitting in what had become his favourite chair looking out of his living-room window.

His shopping trip went surprisingly well. He understood that he was no fashion guru, but he also knew that he wanted to swap his sober navy suits and white shirts for something more reflective of his true character, or at least more reflective of the character that he now understood to be true of him. He would still mostly choose to wear suits; that went without saying, but ones that were less formal, less stiff, less restrictive.

He had not ventured to ask for assistance; that would have been a step too far for his nascent, unfolding personality, but he was satisfied with his purchases. In keeping with the pastel shades of his apartment and the season of the year, he bought a couple of light linen suits with suitably subtly coloured shirts. He did not buy any ties. With a nod to the bright yellow colour that he intended to paint his apartment hallway, he bought a bright yellow polo shirt and white jeans. He did not know when, or even if, he might wear them or whether he would wear them only in the security and privacy of his apartment, but they were a statement that he wanted to make to himself, if not, as yet, to the world.

Longhorne did not know any tunes other than the children's ditty that had so appalled him before his revelation (that seemed an age ago to him and he had not given it any further thought), but if he had he would have hummed one of them to himself as he sat on the bus on his way back home. As it was, he simply sat contentedly, almost dreamily, looking out of the window.

He had stayed in the town centre longer than he had intended; as his bus drew to a halt at his stop the first signs of dusk were beginning to become evident. Alighting from the bus, he started to make his way back to his apartment, but turned at the sound of two police cars on the road, lights flashing and sirens sounding, as they headed out of town at speed. Longhorne's was a quiet neighbourhood where the sound of sirens was an infrequent occurrence. Normally, he would not have turned to observe them but would have continued his way indifferently to his apartment: the business of anyone else was not his business. Now, however, he found himself thinking involuntarily of their mission. Who or

148

what had caused them to flash past? What had happened and to whom? He stood staring into the distance for a moment before turning back again towards home. As he did, he felt a tingle of anticipation at the thought of seeing the child's flowers on his windowsill.

He opened the door to his apartment and walked breezily into his living room, dropping his shopping bags in the hallway rather than taking time to unpack them. They could wait; first of all he had to look at the child's flowers and relive his encounter with her.

They were as he had left them, somewhat incongruously peeking out of his crystal wine decanter. His heart took a little leap and then, without warning, plunged through his body, through his apartment floor, through the earth beneath. A chill stabbed his heart. Disorientated he looked around the room and then back to the flowers. They were screaming at him: something had happened to the child: something wrong, something terrible.

With a jolt he remembered the police cars and their sirens. They had been travelling out of town, out towards his park, out to where he had last seen the little girl and her parents. Something had happened to her there and he had to find out what it was.

All of these thoughts flashed through his mind in an instant. He did not question them; he did not doubt them. He knew simply because he knew, just as he knew that she was not beyond help; not beyond *his* help.

He forced himself to stand still for a moment; instinctively, he closed his eyes and waited. He felt her presence. She was cold, wet, tired, hurt and scared. He felt her fear and he felt the warmth, the life waning slowly from her. He had to act and he had to act straightaway.

He believed that he knew where she was: back in the park where they had met, although how or why she was there he could not tell.

He knew that he had to go to her, not only to rescue her but also to let her know that he *understood*, that the connection she had made with him was more than passing chance. They were bound in some way together, though Longhorne did not quite know how. He understood abstractly that they were one with the Unity, but in his heart he suspected that their bond was specific, fundamental to both of their futures and welfare. It was greater than simply the bond he felt between himself and all life, important as that was.

He turned immediately, hurried out of his apartment and rushed to the bus stop. For the first time in his life, he felt impatience as he waited for the bus to arrive. He paced uneasily from one side of the bus shelter to the other, attracting some wary glances from three or four other people who were also waiting; it was a sign of his agitation that he did not know how many of them there were. Eventually, after what seemed to Longhorne to be half an eternity, the bus drew up and he leapt onboard.

When he arrived at the park, darkness was falling and he found the gates closed. He followed the park fencing until it veered off from the main road and made its way through open woods at the edge of farmland. As he suspected, within a short time, the iron fencing gave way to a chain-link barrier than had fallen into disrepair. Longhorne was reasonably fit; he had no difficulty in climbing over it.

In the gathering gloom, he had no real idea where he was, but he knew that the lake lay at the centre of the park. Once he found that, he would be able to follow the shore until he came to the park bench where he and the little girl had sat a few hours before. He was now as certain as he was of anything in his life that he would find her there.

Finding the lake proved easier than he had thought. With an increased sense of urgency he began to walk clockwise around it. In no time at all, he reassured himself, he would be there. He reached out in his mind to the little girl to reassure her too.

Then it happened again.

This time, Longhorne felt it beginning to happen and tried, in vain, to resist it. He was aware of a fog descending on his mind and his balance beginning to go. He fell to the ground with his face buried in short grass at the edge of a path. As awareness of his surroundings began to fade, incongruously he had time to wonder why on this occasion the transition from his own mind to the mind of the Other had not been abrupt as before.

He pushed the thought from his mind; he did not have time for musing and he did not have time for this interruption. Time was precisely what he didn't have: it was rapidly running out for the little girl. Already he could sense that her heartbeat was weak and her body temperature dangerously low. With a final effort, he tried to shake himself back to normal consciousness, but the mind of the Other was too strong. He had no option; he had to let himself fall into it.

Immediately, he felt the desperation of the Other; he felt the panic and the doubt. With alarm, Longhorne realised that he was back in the garden of Gethsemane, back where he had been at his last encounter with the Other. But why? He had been through this before; what was the point of him experiencing it again? He had a sense that the mind of the Other had controlled his previous experiences, had chosen which moments in the life of Jesus of Nazareth to reveal. He felt instinctively that each revelation was for a purpose; now, with this repetition of events, he was not so sure.

Even as these thoughts flowed through his mind, he realised that this time *was* different. He was aware both of the mind of the other and of his own mind as before; indeed, he seemed to have a sharper ability to monitor, even to question, the experience. Nonetheless, something fundamental had changed. Paradoxically, while being more aware of the separation between his mind and the mind of the Other, he was also aware that the Other's thoughts were much closer to him than before, though he could not previously have believed that such a thing was possible. This time he was not only experiencing the thoughts of the other as the Other's mind flooded his, but he felt that he was an active participant *in* the Other's thoughts. While not exactly forming the Other's thoughts, he was, in some way that he could not begin to explain or understand, associated with their formation.

He was not only being affected by the Other's mind, but the Other's mind was also being affected by his. It was as if the Other was not complete without him, just as he was not complete without the Other.

All the while, Longhorne knew that he was still fully and completely Longhorne, able to think clearly in his own right. He oscillated rapidly between experiencing the Other and reflecting on the experience; more than that, he realised: it seemed to him that he was able to do both simultaneously. He was aware that the Other's mind was being influenced by his, just as he understood that his mind had been flooded by the presence of the Other. He did not feel, however, that his thoughts were being directed or controlled by the Other; the Other had allowed him access to its mind, but it had not transgressed into his. Perhaps this was the work of the Unity; perhaps the Other's mind had no more control than he did over who or what had acccss to it. Perhaps they were both parts of the one mind: the mind of the Unity that encompassed all minds. All of this, he thought in the time that it took him to fall to the ground.

In any event, he knew what to expect; he had been here before. He knew that the panic and the falling into he abyss would be halted as the Unity that lay behind the Other would step in and effect a rescue. Even as he felt the panic and as the abyss looming before him, he felt confident that the experience was going to come to an end with the Unity's intervention. He was eager, impatient for it to happen so he could resume his urgent task of rescuing the little girl. He realised that he knew something that the Other didn't: he was privy to the Other's future. What appeared as a present and critical crisis for the Other was a story that had already been told to Longhorne. He could not help but feel a little smug.

Even as he slipped over the edge of the abyss with the Other, part of him felt aloof from the Other's panic. He felt pity for the Other, but he also felt a pleasing sense of privileged knowledge, bordering on a heady sense of omniscience. He knew, in his heart, that such grandiose thoughts were unwarranted, but he could not deny that he had them. He assuaged his conscience by telling himself that if he was bordering on omniscience, it was only because his mind was flowing within that of the Unity. The omniscience belonged not to him, but it was being reflected within him.

He could not deny it. He knew something that the Other did not know: all would be well; rescue would come.

It didn't.

Thirteen

Longhorne had felt himself falling into an abyss of darkness, sorrow and hopelessness. Even as he did so, he waited for the Unity to intervene, to carry him and the Other back into the light. As the darkness overwhelmed him, he almost savoured it, knowing that it would give way to the indescribable peace that he had experienced before. He invited it to do its worst; the deeper the depression, the sweeter would be the relief.

Instead he felt the darkness close round him, pressing into his mind, holding him in its remorseless grip. His awareness of everything other than the darkness around him began to recede, slowly at first, but then racing away at lightning speed. Not only did the Unity not intervene, but his sense of the Other diminished also until it was only the faintest shade of light in the cloud of darkness that enveloped him, Finally, it also disappeared totally from his consciousness and he was alone; totally and completely alone.

He was alone and fearful, trapped by a force that he could not defend himself against, a force that he could neither understand nor wrestle. All thoughts of the Other and the Unity disappeared from his mind as if snatched away by an invisible hand. They could not help him, they could not intervene: there was no light at the end of the tunnel; there was no rescue to be had.

He felt crushed as if the entire weight of the Earth was pressing him down, pressing him against an invisible barrier, pressing him so that all life would be squeezed from his body, from his soul. The darkness swirled around him, hot and full of flame and violence, full of menace and terror. It encapsulated everything that was opposed to him, to his existence. It wanted to attack him, to negate him, to smash him and blot him out as if he had never been. It screamed at him and he screamed back, it thundered against him and he howled at it, it broke against him time and again as mountainous seas might break against crumbling cliffs. He crumpled, broken and exhausted with the fight. He let go, he abandoned himself to it; he could do nothing else. He lay defenceless before it, without hope, without heart, without life.

The roar of the darkness stopped; now it whispered to him, pressing ever closer, enveloping and shrouding his mind. Now it felt cool, almost soothing. He could no longer think of anything other than its presence; it merged with his mind and soul, it infiltrated the fabric and fibre of his being, until he could not identify it as something extrinsic to him. It was no longer his enemy, his assailant. It had stopped beating him; instead it wrapped its arms around him. The darkness was no longer outside him and he began to wonder if it ever had been. It was inside him. Slowly, hesitantly he welcomed it. It expanded, filling his mind completely until he accepted that the darkness was not only within him; it *was* him.

The blind, naked panic that had earlier rushed through his body and mind was gone as if it had never been. With deliberation, he accepted that there could be no escape from the darkness any more than there could be an escape from himself. He realised with a complete certainty that the abyss that he had been falling into was an abyss at the heart of himself. Instead of recoiling from the thought, he embraced it; he was who and what he was.

With this confession, the darkness unexpectedly disappeared as if it had been nothing more than a mist, to be replaced by something that Longhorne could only describe as *nothing*. There was no colour or absence of colour. There was no sound or absence of sound. There was no feeling or absence of feeling. There was no thought or absence of thought. There was neither light nor darkness. There was nothing.

All that remained was Being; beyond thought, beyond feeling and beyond sense. It was pure Being and it was formless and void. Intuitively, he knew that it was also eternal; not stretching before him as an endless road to be travelled, but simply there: an eternal instant that encapsulated all that there was. Longhorne could not think, he could not feel; he simply was and what he was... was nothing. He was without time, without space; without body or mind; he was eternal and he was a moment: he was.

He knew now that he was finally experiencing himself: his true self, stripped of everything that was not him, and he knew who and what he was. He was nothing: formless, empty, void. He felt no panic, no despair; he felt nothing. He was alone in the Universe. With certain knowledge, he understood that he was alone because he *was* the Universe and in the Universe there was nothing except his emptiness.

His emptiness, his nothingness was a place where he belonged. It asked nothing of him, it made no demands and it had no expectations. It would be wrong to say that Longhorne enjoyed it or that he found it comforting; the experience went beyond emotion. In this state, he knew that emotions were unnecessary, redundant, non-existent. Rather, he experienced a sense of completeness, of oneness, because he and he alone existed. There was no struggle, no questioning, no pain; nor was there joy, hope or love. There was simply Being and that was something so sublimely empty, so fundamentally *nothing* that it made everything else, good or bad, superfluous.

He sensed that in this state of Being, he too no longer existed. *Being* existed, but Longhorne as an individual, as something apart from pure Being, did not. There was no Longhorne, there was no Universe, there was nothing and *nothing* was more perfect than the greatest perfection that he could ever have previously imagined. Nothing went beyond thought or consciousness; it transcended anything that words could describe or hope to explain. It was nowhere and everywhere, it was now and always, it was nothing.

It came to an end.

Later, he came to understand that it was not accurate to say that it ended: rather, his *experience* of his eternal moment came to an end. Even as it did so, he also knew that it continued to be, though no longer on a plane accessible to him. Somewhere, nowhere, pure Being was, but he was no longer privy to it.

Into his nothingness, a voice spoke. He knew that it was not his own voice for he had no voice and even if he had, he had no thoughts to think, no words to say. With the intrusion of the voice came the need to think, to respond. With it came the erosion of pure Being; with it came consciousness of another and so consciousness of himself. With it came distinction and relation; with it came joy and sorrow.

Already, the voice brought him pain; pain at the loss of his experience of pure Being, pain at the loss of existing as nothing. He resented it and in the act of resenting, he knew that he had lost everything that nothing had offered him. Back came thoughts, words, feelings; back came a reality that existed beyond the reality of nothing.

The voice offered him a choice: to return to the eternity of his nothingness or to surrender to *it*; to surrender to the voice. He wanted immediately to fall back into nothing, into the fullness and the emptiness that it gave him. He wanted to fall back into the wholeness of being that not being Longhorne gave him; he wanted just to be.

The voice spoke only once. It did not ask or plead or negotiate. It simply offered him a choice: to follow it or not. To follow it meant the loss of *nothing*; to reject it meant the gain of nothing. Longhorne knew that he had all the time in eternity to make his choice; that no matter how long he pondered, his decision would take forever and it would take an instant.

Into his mind came an image. It was not created by the voice nor was it an image of the voice, but it had within it the resonance of the voice. It had within it also a resonance both of his own mind and soul: he saw the face of the little girl.

At once his mind was made up. He did not know the origin of the voice, but if it was associated with the little girl who had touched his soul, he wanted to know it, he needed to know it and if that meant following it, so be it. Words formed in his mind and he gave his affirmation.

The voice did not reply. It did not thank him or praise him for his decision. Longhorne could sense that it was satisfied with his response, but that also it would have allowed him to decline its invitation without rancour or disapproval. It was not that the voice was neutral, but rather that it was on his side regardless of his decision. It was irrevocably *for* him. At the same time, he also knew that his decision was equally irrevocable. There was no going back; his route to nothing was closed forever and while somewhere or nowhere his eternal moment still existed, he was no longer with it.

Just as quickly as the darkness had rushed upon him prior to his moment of eternity, it filled his mind once more. He knew that it would be so, that it had to be so, but it appalled him nonetheless. He knew that the darkness came from within him and that he had refused to escape from it by refusing to choose nothing, but this did not diminish the grief and anguish that he felt. As it rolled upon him, wave after wave, he recognised that there was even more to the darkness than his own soul, but what it was he could not fathom.

He knew that the only way to break free from the pain and despair that he was feeling was for the Unity to intervene, but nothing was happening. How long was he to wait for the Unity to rescue him? Did he have to endure an eternity, lost in the darkness?

As the darkness closed ever more tightly around him, he struggled to think. He feared that he would lose his mind and be trapped forever in it when instinctively he turned for help from the voice that had spoken to him in and from eternity. He realised that it was there, waiting with eternal patience for him to turn to it. It did not intervene, he now understood; it participated.

At once the darkness lifted, the pain receded and he felt the indescribable presence of the Unity as he had done previously. As relief flooded over him, it took a few moments to realise that the voice and the Unity were the same. He allowed himself to enjoy the peace that he now felt, but unlike his experience of the eternal nothing, he knew that he was not to linger there.

As if he were in a film that was playing backwards, he sensed the presence of the Other as he fought his own battle in the Garden of Gethsemane. This time, Longhorne felt less like a spectator or passive participant in the Other's experience: he felt like a kindred spirit.

They had endured and enjoyed the same trial, they had come to the same decision: they were brothers.

Captivating as this insight was, Longhorne knew that he would have to return to it later to ponder its significance. The face of the little girl was before him again and as he moved closer to regaining his normal consciousness, her plight grew ever more insistent.

He could see her face, white in the moonlight that now bathed the park. He could see that she was not moving, not breathing. With an effort, he concentrated his focus on her completely. He could sense the bond between them, he could touch her mind and soul, but he could not sense a heartbeat within her. He knew that she was dying, teetering on the borderline between life and death and he knew that he had to reach her now. With a supreme effort, he forced his eyes to open.

Fourteen

Longhorne was lying face down in short grass at the side of the path that ran around the park's lake. He felt the grass wet on his face from the dew that had descended. He could not tell how long he had been in his trance, but night had fallen fully, a bright moon was high in the sky and a gentle chilly breeze was blowing across the lake.

He stood abruptly to his feet, caught his bearings and began to run as fast as he could along the path. He wasn't sure how far away the little girl was, but he knew that if he followed the path he would come to the point where he and the child had met.

Rounding a bend in the path, he saw her, lying on the park bench where they had sat together a few hours earlier. He rushed to her side and dropping to his knees began to feel the side of her neck for a pulse. To his alarm, he was unable to detect one. He brought his cheek close to her mouth to see if he could find any sign of breathing, but again he detected nothing. She was stone cold to his touch, but in spite of this and her lack of pulse and breathing, he sensed that life had not completely left her body; he did not know quite how, but he was sure of it.

Longhorne did not know any resuscitation techniques. He had never considered it likely that he would be in a position to use them and had taken no interest in finding out anything about them. Why would he have troubled himself with learning how to intervene in the lives of others, even if they were in need of his help? What had they to do with him or he with them? Now he chided himself for his insularity even as his mind raced to find a solution to his present predicament. He knew that he had to do something; he could not permit himself simply to kneel there helplessly if there was some hope, however small, that the child's life might still be saved. As one part of his mind sought frantically to find a way to act, another part warned him that he could easily harm her further if he made the wrong intervention. Instead of helping her, he could remove any faint chance of recovery that she might have.

As his mental tug-of-war paralysed him, he shouted in frustration. An almost animal howl erupted viscerally from within him, roaring through his chest like the fires of a violent volcano. His howl echoed across the lake, returning to him as if in mockery of his impotence. What was he to do? He had to act; he had been alerted to the little girl's predicament for a reason and that had to be to save her life. Why else had he been drawn from his apartment living room to seek her in the park? It certainly wasn't to kneel helplessly at the dying child's side.

With a supreme effort, he forced himself to suppress the panic and the frustration; he had to think. As his mind calmed, he realised that he had vague memories of reading something about resuscitation in some book or other, but even as his hopes rose, he recognised that they were much too ill-formed and fleeting to be of any use. He tried to think harder, to see the image of the page of the book that he must have read, but nothing further would come to him. All the while, he knew that life continued to drain from the little girl; his panic began to rise again.

As tears of anger began to sting his eyes, the thought came to him that he was not to try to reason his way to a solution; he had to act on instinct, on feeling. He felt himself letting go of the control that he exercised over his mind and actions; he moved in response to something deeper than rational thought, something more fundamental. He took off his jacket and placed it on the grass. He lifted the child gently from the bench and placed her on it. He then laid his body over hers, his hands touching hers, his chest on hers, his mouth over hers.

He closed his eyes and made the connection. He could feel her life, her soul within; still there like a small candle in a cold dark room. He willed the flickering candle flame to hold fast, to refuse to be snuffed out; he willed it to continue to burn and then to burn stronger, brighter; slowly in response to his will, it did. He began to push air from his lungs into hers and the flame grew brighter still until it was no longer the flame of a candle, but a small fire. Finally with a roar it burst into life, filling the room with warmth and light as if it were feeding on the oxygen that he was forcing into the child's lungs. Triumphantly, Longhorne raised his mouth from the child's. She stirred, looked at him with recognition, with communion, with love. He knelt above her, tears of relief streaming down his face, mixing freely with the perspiration of his exertions. The light from the fire of her soul seemed to be all around him, filling the night with its light. He raised his hands in joy, he raised his voice in a shout of victory, he raised his face to the moon.

They started punching and kicking him.

Longhorne had been so totally engrossed in the plight of the little girl and his need to rescue her that he had not seen the torch-beams or heard the calls of the search party as it made its way through the park. They had been searching for some hours, expanding their circle from the little girl's home some two miles away when, having reached the edge of the park, they had been alerted by the shouts of despair that had burst from him as he sought a way to help the dying child. As they came upon him, straddling the child, they hoped that they had caught him in time, but they feared the worst.

No one knew quite how or why the little girl had managed to escape her parents' attention twice in one day, but late in the afternoon they had become aware that she was no longer playing in the back garden of their home. At first, assured that she must have been close to home, they were irritated more by their lack of vigilance than by her lack of awareness of the distress that her earlier disappearance had caused. She had shown no understanding that she might have placed herself in danger by wandering off in the park and as they had tried to hide their concerns from her they could not fault her for wandering again. Still, they thought that it was unusual that she should have done so; it had never been a problem for them before. They chided one another and determined to speak to her firmly once she had been found.

Their irritation turned to alarm as they looked around their home and then their immediate neighbourhood in vain. In disbelief, they realised that she was gone: the police cars that had flashed past Longhorne's apartment were responding to their frightened call for help.

As with many such incidents, the police took their time to ascertain facts and to rule out simple solutions before beginning a search of the neighbourhood. The child's parents had mentioned the earlier incident in the park and had given the police a description of Longhorne, but the officers that dealt with their call were loath to jump to conclusions, to connect the little girl's disappearance with him. The parents had offered no information that led them to think that he had followed her from the park to their home. The distance for their home to the park was thought to be too great for the little girl to have walked on her own so they assumed, as had her parents, that she must have been closer to home. Proper protocols had to be observed.

Time passed quickly as they followed their routine procedure. Only as darkness threatened to fall, did they enlist the help of friends and neighbours and call for reinforcements as they, too, began to worry that something was seriously wrong. Quietly, they asked for medical assistance to be at hand.

As the search party's circle grew ever wider and as more and more people joined in the search, they eventually came to the edge of the locked park. Thinking that it was unlikely that the child could have got through the fence the searchers were about to skirt round the perimeter when they heard Longhorne's cry. The first group climbed the fence while others alerted the police.

A group of four men were the first to see Longhorne kneeling over the child's body. Three of them wrestled him to the ground and began to kick and punch him while the fourth scooped the child into his arms. Relieved that she was breathing, though cold and wet, he handed her over to police officers, who had arrived, panting, on the scene. Two of them hurried her back to the park entrance where paramedics were waiting. The others rescued Longhorne from his attackers, hand-cuffed him and dragged him to the park gates, where they bundled him into a police car before other members of the search party could turn their anger against him into violent reprisal.

No one ever found out the exact circumstances that led to the little girl being in the park and so a series of unanswered questions were endlessly debated. Had she made her way to the park of her own accord or had she been enticed there by Longhorne? Was this a planned assault on the child or was it an opportunist crime? Had he been interrupted from abducting her earlier in the day by her parents or had he been grooming her for a later occasion? No one knew, but everyone had a theory. From the state of her clothes, it was apparent that she had walked or had been dragged through rough undergrowth. The fact that she was soaked to the skin even though it had not been raining suggested that she had been in the lake at some point, but how or why, again, no one could be sure. She bore no bruises and had no signs of having been physically attacked, but her parents, the police and the search party were of no doubt that Longhorne had somehow managed to lure her from her home to the park and had been in the process of attacking her when he was interrupted by the search party.

Soon, word of the abduction spread throughout the neighbourhood, TV news crews arrived and the story was taken up by local and then national media. By breakfast time, the little girl's ordeal was national news and community leaders, politicians and police officials were being interviewed by a host of reporters on a series of programmes. Longhorne's identity had not been released to the media, but he was presented as an example of depravity, an instant hate figure who had abducted not only an innocent child, but a child with Down's syndrome. Why that made the abduction worse, no one ventured to say, but all agreed that it had made his crime all the more heinous.

Throughout, the child said nothing and was unresponsive to questioning by the trained police officers and medical staff that attended her. She seemed to be blissfully unaware that she had been through any ordeal or that she was the centre of a national news story. She was pleased to be re-united with her parents, who were soon able to bring her back home, but gave no sign to them that she had been frightened or upset by her experiences. Of Longhorne, she said nothing, but smiled once or twice when they spoke of 'the man in the park'. Very quickly, they stopped mentioning the incident and began to act as if it had never happened. They were chastened by their experience, but vented their anger and frustration not at themselves for their carelessness, but at Longhorne whom they were certain had somehow managed to abduct and attack their child.

They, and thousands of others, would see that he paid for his crime.

Fifteen

Longhorne spent a sleepless night in a police cell. He was alone even though a number of the other cells were full to capacity. The police understood well enough that the cause of his arrest and the nature of his crime (for crime it surely was) would filter through to the other inmates; they also understood fully how he would be treated by them. While having no sympathy for him, they could ill afford to have an assault or even a murder take place while he was in their custody and there was good reason to think that either could happen. They satisfied themselves by throwing him into his cell with a little rough handling thrown in for good measure; the police doctor that they would be obliged to call would not be able to distinguish their calling cards from the cuts and bruises left by his assailants in the park.

And so it proved to be: the doctor found that a still and silent Longhorne had sustained multiple injuries to his face, torso and limbs, but they were relatively minor; none, in his professional opinion, required hospital attention. He left a few painkillers at the front desk, but they weren't offered to him by the officers on duty and even if they had been, Longhorne would have had no interest in taking them. His mind and attention were elsewhere.

As the police had anticipated, the occupants of other cells quickly discovered why he had been arrested and, in the nature of such things, as the word was passed from cell to cell, details were added and they became convinced that the child had died under his attack. They hurled abuse at him, threatening to avenge the child if only they could get their hands on him. Emboldened by their sense of relative self-righteousness, they called for rough justice to be meted out, each inmate outdoing the others in volunteering to be executioner. Longhorne remained as oblivious of them and their threats as he was of his injuries.

He understood that he was in deep trouble, but he also knew that he was totally innocent of any wrongdoing; even more innocent, he told himself, than he had been in the events that had led to his parents' deaths. The thought mattered little to him; this time his attitude was different. He was not interested in either proving his innocence or avoiding whatever actions the police or the courts might choose to take. He was content to let them take their course. He simply did not care.

He knew that he had saved the little girl's life and he also knew that no one would believe him. He understood that any account that he might give of the prescience that led him to the park to look for her, any account of his subsequent actions in resuscitating her and any account of the sense of the fundamental connectedness that he felt with her because of their mutual oneness with the Unity, would fall on deaf ears. He did not expect that the child would be able to speak in his favour or even be able to recount what had happened to her. His fate, he knew, was sealed.

But he had saved a life; not just a life: he had saved *her* life and that was all that mattered. One life saved, *her* life saved, was worth whatever price he had to pay.

Longhorne was sleepless, not because he was anxious or fearful; he did not sleep because he had never felt more alive, more able to understand who and what he was. At last, after many iterations, he felt that he had come to the final version of himself: the true Longhorne had emerged. He recognised that his existence had meaning and that meaning had been brought to fruition. He existed in order to save the life of the little girl in the park. Everything else in his life up to that point and everything that might come after was ancillary to that one great purpose: he had *saved* her; he had saved *her*.

She was the most precious thing in the Universe to him because she was the only one of *her* that existed and he had found her; more correctly, she had found him. Longhorne knew that, in theory, he could have said the same about anyone, but that would have been to miss the point. He recognised that every person was uniquely and equally precious, but he had been awakened to *her* unique presence. It was, no doubt, the task and the joy of others to be awakened to those around them, but he had fulfilled his task: he had touched the essence of her soul; he had known its beauty and wonder. More than that, he had known her love, unspoken, unconditional, unwarranted. The knowledge of one life was enough for him; the knowledge that he had saved one life was a bonus he had neither expected nor felt he had merited. Whatever might happen to him, the sacrifice would be worth it. He had been saved by her: saved from a solitary existence, saved through the gift she had given him of allowing him to sacrifice himself for her.

He had no idea what might become of her, whether she would live to a ripe old age or die tragically young. He did not know if she would live what others might consider to be a fulfilled life or whether she would inhabit the twilight and the shadows. He didn't know or care if she would retain her sweet nature or become cramped and narrow as she navigated life. It did not matter: he could only act on what he knew now and what he knew was that she was infinitely precious and he had saved her just as she had saved him.

He understood that his actions were not entirely altruistic and yet he also understood that they were not selfish; they were simply *right*. For the first time in his life, he knew that he had done the right thing simply and purely because it was the right thing to do and he was satisfied. He was whole.

Waves of satisfaction broke over him, threatening to border again on ecstasy. He felt that his heart would burst, that he needed to open the top of his skull to relieve the pressure of sheer happiness that he felt pounding through his brain. He had had no idea that life could be like this. He had no thought of the morning or what it might bring; he was literally careless.

He spent the best night of his life, alone in a concrete cell surrounded by people baying for his blood; he had never been happier.

The police left him to languish in his cell long after the other cells had been emptied and their residents either tossed back sober unto the street or brought to court for arraignment. They brought him coffee and a plain breakfast around 8am, but he was not interested in eating or drinking. They escorted him to the bathroom, telling him to clean himself up for a court appearance sometime later in the morning. Apart from brushing his teeth and washing his hands and face, he made no attempt to make himself presentable; he did not care that his trousers and jacket were stained and crumpled, that the collar of his shirt was torn or that his hair was dirty with mud and blood. His outward appearance, something that he had been fastidious about for more than a decade, meant nothing to him now.

His appearance became a topic of conversation among the police officers that arrived for the day shift. They were aware of the news reports and knew that they would have to present him to a judge. They were as certain as everyone else that he was guilty of child abduction and that he had been stopped just in time before assaulting and perhaps killing his victim. They did not want any possible cause for sympathy or any reason for judicial doubt to enter the judge's mind. They were concerned that his matted hair, his torn and dirty clothing, and his pale, almost haggard, features might suggest that they had offered him inadequate care overnight, that they had made no attempt to seek his welfare, that they had already acted as judge and jury and had found him guilty. That all of this was, indeed, true was irrelevant; justice must be seen to be done.

After some deliberation they decided that he should be dressed in prison-style overalls; they had an ample supply of them. They would explain that they had rescued him from being beaten by the men that had found him and his victim, that his clothes had been too badly torn for him to wear. He made no protest when they ordered him to strip or when they added a few extra tears to his clothing to complement their story. He made no comment at their shocked exclamations at seeing the scars on his back or at their ribald jokes as he stood naked in the shower and he complied silently as they swore at him, urging him to hurry as he dressed.

He was silent throughout, just as he had been when they had initially read him his rights, just as he had been when they asked him if he wanted to phone for legal assistance, just as he had been when a public lawyer had visited him.

Then they waited.

By the time they got the call to bring him to the local courthouse, it was already past noon and they realised that a considerable police presence was needed both outside the station where he was being held and at the courthouse where he was to be taken for his initial hearing. Large crowds had gathered around both venues;

not just the press and TV news crews, but mobs of angry citizens. The police toyed with the idea of conducting the hearing via a video link, but the judge dismissed the idea; Longhorne might have tried to commit a reprehensible crime under the cover of darkness, but he would face justice in the daylight of a public court.

After some delay while discussions took place and preparations were made, he was bundled into the back of an armoured van at the rear of the police station and driven at speed with an escort to the courthouse where the crowd had been pushed back by a cordon of officers. As he stepped out of the van he was met with howls of protest. A bottle, then another, then a hail of objects landed at his feet and littered his wake as he was raced up the steps of the building and into the safety of the foyer. He was quickly inspected for any fresh signs of injury before being marched into the courtroom, where the press and public galleries were packed to capacity. He was brought straight to the raised dock, where his handcuffs were taken off. The officers accompanying him stood either side and a little behind him, tense and ready as if they expected him either to make a run for it or to launch himself at the judge.

Neither action could have been further from his mind.

Longhorne was not on trial; this was merely an initial arraignment at which the judge would decide if there was sufficient reason for him to be brought to trial at a later date. Her primary task was to determine if the police had sufficient cause to charge him with the abduction and assault on the little girl, who was referred to simply as 'Child T'. If she agreed that they had, she would have to determine whether he should be allowed to return to his home on bail or whether he should continue to be detained until his trial.

The police officers presenting their case admitted that they had no idea who Longhorne was. He had carried no identification with him when he had gone to the park and he had not spoken a word to them since his arrest. His fingerprints might be on file, but a thorough search had not yet been conducted and might take some time. Similarly, they were not, as yet, able to trace him from the photographs that they had taken in the police station. Neither the men who had rescued his victim nor the little girl's parents recognised him other than to confirm that he was the same man who had been with their daughter earlier in the day. His identity was a mystery. Had his crime not stirred up such popular interest and anger, they would have waited until a formal identification had been made before bringing him to court, but they deemed it to be in the public interest to act quickly. He could be charged under a pseudonym, if necessary; the paperwork would follow.

When asked to state his name, Longhorne remained silent. He was not being obstructive or defiant; he was simply not present. His mind continued to be elsewhere as the court rituals continued. His surroundings were receding from him, becoming increasingly hazy, almost ethereal, as the clarity of his 'mission' imposed itself on his mind. He found it difficult to focus on the courtroom, on the crowded galleries, on his guards; even on the judge. He could see her lips move, he could hear sounds coming from her mouth, but they made no sense to him. He did not reply to her repeated questioning not because he refused to, but because he was unable to.

As the reality of the courtroom dissolved before him, the presence of the Other and the all-encompassing reality of the Unity became ever more apparent. He felt joined to them in a new and deeper way; he felt one with them as fully as he believed it was possible to be.

It was all because of the little girl. She had been the last link in the chain that had brought him to this point. She had enabled him to make true contact with another embodied soul, she had enabled him to reach out to another life, she had enabled him to fulfil his mission.

The hearing continued around him; without him. He was less than a witness to the proceedings, less even than the little girl would have been had she been present. Yet she was present. He was absent from his surroundings because he was with her, with the Other, with the Unity. The police offered their evidence, the judge pronounced that there was more than sufficient evidence against him to warrant his arrest and continued detention; there was, she agreed, no question of a dangerous, unknown man being allowed bail even if he were able to secure it.

The judge launched into a speech detailing the seriousness of the charges that Longhorne would have to face, the depravity of the acts he had been accused of, the severity of the penalty he would pay if he were to be found guilty of them and the lasting harm that had been inflicted on his victim and her parents. Longhorne's inattention at first disturbed her, then irritated her, then finally frustrated and infuriated her. She warned him of the consequences of refusing to cooperate with the court, she berated him for his insolence and arrogance, she gave him a final chance to speak for himself. Getting nothing in return, she washed her hands of him as the crowd in the public gallery became increasingly restive and then vocal in their opposition to him. A voice called for him to locked up and the key thrown away; another shouted that the death penalty would be too good for him. Others joined in until the judge decided that she had let things slide enough and called the court back to order.

As a hush descended on the room and the press stopped their scribbling, she looked Longhorne in the eye and in a half-whisper commanded the guards to take him away.

Longhorne took in none of this. He had reached the point of no return. It was done; it was finished. He had fulfilled his mission, he had attained oneness with this single life and in so doing had attained oneness with the Other, with the Unity, with all things. In saving her, he had, himself, been saved. Her life had become his life and together their lives had become part of all life. In saving her, he had saved all that was and in being saved, he had been embraced by all that ever could be. He was satisfied; he was whole. In saying 'yes' to her instead of choosing *nothing*, he had spoken the final word; more than that, he realised that he *was* the final word. Nothing further remained to be said.

Oblivious now of all around him, he involuntarily raised both his hands aloft. The guards by his side moved forward, fearful that he was going to make some grand gesture, perhaps even propel himself from his wooden enclosure. Unaware of them, unaware of everything other than the feelings of peace and relief that filled his mind, he fell to the floor as the aneurysm in his brain burst. Within seconds he was unconscious and within minutes he was dead.

Sixteen

The autopsy indicated that the aneurysm that had been growing in Longhorne's brain had been there for only a short time, perhaps as little as a week or two. It had developed rapidly and had resulted in a massive bleed that had made his death both swift and inevitable. There was no evidence that its rupture had been either caused or hastened by the blows that he had suffered the previous night; it was inevitable that it would have burst unless it had been treated surgically. Even then, the outcome would have been uncertain.

There was a brief, unresolved debate regarding whether or not the aneurysm might have contributed to Longhorne's behaviour in abducting the small girl and attacking her in the park. That he *had* abducted her was beyond question: his actions were universally reported and interpreted in this manner by the press and public alike. No other explanation of his behaviour was offered or sought.

The public got what the public wanted. In the absence of a trial, he was found irrevocably guilty at the bar of popular opinion. The little girl's family eschewed further publicity and this served only to add to the rumour mill that rapidly supplied prurient details of Longhorne's supposed activities on the night of his arrest. Some asserted that he had completed his attack before the child's rescuers had arrived to stop him killing her, others that he had been stopped en route to a secret hide-away where he was going to keep the child. Many created a back-story for him, suggesting that he had stalked the child for some time or that he had been guilty of similar attacks over a number of years.

The press and TV news focused most of their interest on his final moments in court: all agreed that his death was both deserved and timely. He dominated media headlines for a day or two and then the story was archived. A few commentators of religious persuasion declared that his death in court had been a sign of divine judgement, not only on him but on all such offenders. Their opinions were sanctified or ignored according to their audience's particular predilections. The little girl's rescuers enjoyed brief celebrity and then faded from view as public attention moved elsewhere. Within a few days, the world went on as if Longhorne had never been.

While, at an undetermined future date, an inquest was to be held into his death, there was no expectation that either the police or the men who had apprehended him would, as a result, be charged with any crime or found guilty of any misconduct. It was thought unlikely that there would be any media interest in the inquest; Longhorne had come rapidly into public view and the public wanted just as rapidly to rid themselves of him. He had served his purpose in supplying an opportunity for an outpouring of righteous indignation; he was of no more use to anyone.

Once the cause of death had been determined, his body was released by the coroner, but the authorities were presented with an immediate problem: they had no one to contact regarding his death. They had been able to establish his identity quite quickly as a result of their fingerprint search which had enabled them to trace him to the farmhouse fire of a decade earlier. At much the same time, his employers supplied limited further information after they had responded to a photograph that had been published in the press and on social media, but neither a subsequent police search of his apartment (which, to their minds, confirmed his eccentricities) nor a detailed examination of the file on his previous trial had given them any details of living next of kin. Under these circumstances, it was their responsibility to dispose of his body, but they were keen to explore every avenue to see if they could find someone who would lay claim to his remains; protocols and process had to be followed even if no one cared.

To that effect, some days after his death, the authorities attempted to stir up some additional interest in him by employing a journalist to write his story. It outlined his final crime and his previous, solitary way of life. It recounted his appearance in court following the devastating fire that had brought an end to his adoptive parents' lives. Neither officialdom nor the journalist had been able to discover his natural mother's identity; the legal paper trail had no record of her, but appeared to begin and end with his adoption by the middle-aged couple who became his parents. They had intervened when he was only a few weeks old, but their deaths meant that whatever else they might have known about him, that knowledge died with them. His father's sister had also died in the intervening years and her compliant husband had followed her to the grave. They had lived and died childless. The orphanage that was listed in his adoption papers had given Longhorne the name 'John', but there was no reference to a surname or any suggestion that John had been his birth name The investigation into his original identity ran into the sand.

The journalist had discovered and duly reported that Longhorne had attended Church schools in the town near his adoptive parents' home, but as interest in the story had rapidly waned, she decided that trying to contact any of his former teachers or fellow pupils for comment was not worth the effort. His employers and fellow workers had nothing of note to say about him following his death; it was improbable that contacts from longer ago would provide any further enlightenment. Her task was to produce a story that would enable any existing relatives to claim his body. That was the job she had been paid for and that was the job she was prepared to do; nothing less, but certainly nothing more. Her story ended with an appeal, stating that if someone could prove a close connection to Longhorne, they could take charge of his burial or cremation with the costs being borne by the state. A local government official would accompany Longhorne's body throughout to ensure that it was not handed over to crank or malicious claimants. Like the rest of the world, the journalist moved on to other things.

A smattering of replies resulted: some from former teachers, some from former pupils of the schools that Longhorne had attended. Almost invariably, they commented that they had not really known him, that he had been a loner and that they were not surprised when they heard that he had met the end that he had. There were no expressions of friendship, of regret or of sorrow. Nothing emerged that provided either new information on Longhorne's past or a resolution to the disposal of his body.

Just as the authorities were prepared to give up hope of finding someone to claim his body and were resigned to disposing of it themselves, a woman in her mid-forties contacted them. She was not certain, but she thought that he might be her son.

Her story was a sad one, but for those who listened to her, who took notes as she talked and who reported to their superiors, it was by no means unique. They had heard and seen most things, not just once or twice, but too often to remember, too often to be shocked, too often to care too much.

She had given up her child, a boy, for 'rescue' thirty-one years ago. When she was fifteen years old, she had been raped by her uncle, her father's brother; a favourite who often stayed at their home. He had found a job overseas and the family were celebrating his success before he left to take up his new position. Fuelled with alcohol, he had stumbled into her bedroom and attacked her while the rest of the household slept. He had never approached her before. He had never acted inappropriately before. He had never touched her before. He would never do so again.

He left the next morning.

Too embarrassed, ashamed and shocked to say anything to her parents, she absorbed her revulsion and tried to push the incident away from her consciousness until months later she discovered that she was pregnant. Distressed, humiliated and fearful, she told her parents of her uncle's attack, of her confusion that followed, of her vain attempts to make the memories go away.

They refused to believe her.

They accused her of having 'slept around', of being immoral, of bringing shame on them and of telling outrageous lies against an innocent man, a man who was loved and respected by all in the family, a man who, in turn, had only ever shown her love and kindness. Her attempts to cover her blatant wantonness with malicious lies were reprehensible.

Nonetheless, they would stand by her, although they pointed out constantly that she didn't deserve their support, especially in the light of her unwarranted attack on her uncle. Her parents were religious and while they were appalled at her actions, they would not countenance an abortion under any circumstances. They did not want to know the identity of the child's father *even if* she knew which of her secret boyfriends he was and they were adamant that the father would never know of her pregnancy.

They kept 'her condition' a secret for as long as they could and then sent her to an aunt's home, across the country, for the summer, where she was kept under wraps until the baby was born. They had arranged for the child to be taken from her immediately after the birth and left outside a hospital some miles away. Her father had served in the army and had approached the resolution of 'the problem' as if he were conducting a military operation. All involved were sworn to secrecy, all knew the parts they had to play and all pledged never to speak of 'it' again.

She had returned home at the end of the summer and resumed school without any of her friends knowing what had happened. She told them that she had stayed with her aunt over the summer because she needed help with a new baby. Why she imposed that particular cruelty on herself, she never understood, but her parents plan worked: no one knew; no one suspected anything. She too was sworn to secrecy, swallowed her bitterness and pain, bided her time and left home at the earliest opportunity. She found old newspaper reports of an abandoned child being found safely, but after that she had been unable to trace what had become of him, fearful of investigating too closely in case somehow her parents would find out.

She pursued her studies at university, got a job that she liked and had a good circle of friends. Slowly, but deliberately she loosened ties with her family until eventually she cut off all contact with them, refusing to answer their letters, phone calls or emails. Her father once called at her home late one Friday evening; she let him stand outside all night, waiting until he left the next morning before emerging herself, feeling cleansed from her parents' presence and influence.

She abandoned all interest in their religion.

She had heard that her uncle had died in a car crash a few years after she had left home; any thoughts that she had harboured of bringing him to justice had gone. She lit a candle in a local church to mark his death, snuffed it out and walked from the building without looking back.

She could not say why she thought that Longhorne might be her son, but his age and the fact that he had been adopted gave her some cause for belief. It was not that, however, that pushed her to make contact; she simply had a persistent, unshakeable feeling, a determined inner sense, that he was hers.

The authorities were not interested in her inner feelings or intuitions, but concluded that there was some chance that she might be right. They arranged a maternal DNA test which, to their relief, returned a positive result. They were free from their burden; duty had been done. His body was released into her custody and in the circumstances, the requirement for a 'minder' was dropped.

In the interests of her privacy, they kept her story hidden from the press, filed an official report and contented themselves that they had acted dutifully in the public interest by later relating, at Longhorne's inquest, that a relative had been found who had claimed his body. No one took any notice.

She did not know if she should mourn his death or mourn his life. She did not know if she should grieve for him or for herself. How different might his life have been if she had been allowed to keep him? How different would hers?

Still, she mourned, sitting alone all night keeping vigil at his coffin. Thirty years of real memories became supplanted by thirty years of infused memories: memories of what might have been. To her they seemed as true, perhaps even more true, than the record her rational mind recognised and acknowledged. They were colourful, nuanced, hopeful; reality was cold, anaemic… *magnolia*.

She sat alone with him, she mourned alone, but she did not feel alone. She believed that she felt his presence, his life, his soul. She knew that these were but feelings, that they might dispel with the morning light, but she did not care. She had found him and she was his. She felt her love for him and that was enough.

In the morning, before the normal schedule got underway at the crematorium, she took him there. There was no ceremony, no tribute. She was the only one present.

Afterwards she sat with his ashes and pondered what she should do. His ashes held no particular interest for her. He was now locked in her heart; she needed no urn to remind her of that. His presence with her was immovable; he would never again be erased from her life.

She knew from the police enquiries that he had gone weekly to the park for a decade or more. She determined that she would spread his ashes at the lakeside, without seeking permission from the park authorities; a final thumbing of her nose at the propriety that had shaped her life and had imprisoned her for so long, but no longer.

On the morning after his cremation, she made her way to the park as soon as the gates were opened and walked until she found a spot well away from the entrance, close, as it happened, to where her son had met the little girl. A slight breeze was blowing as she scattered his ashes on the lake surface. She sat for a few minutes on the park bench where her son had sat, where his life had found its fulfilment.

She turned and walked away.

Most of Longhorne's ashes drifted along the lake shore, but some caught in the breeze and were lifted into the air. A few particles, almost too small to notice, soared high above the others and were carried far in the winds.

Half a continent away, a weary streetworker, exhausted from her night's toil, slumped against a lamp-post as she made her way home in the dawn light. Suddenly, she looked down sharply at her hand as she felt a prickling, burning sensation… almost like a sting.